Oldham
Council

26. Oct. 22		

Please return this book before the last date stamped.
Items can be renewed by telephone, in person at any library or online at
www.oldham.gov.uk/libraries

Published 2018 by Joffe Books, London.

www.joffebooks.com

ISBN- 978-1-78931-014-6

For my parents, Harry and May. If they were still around, I know they would be proud.

Prologue

The man paused in the hallway, checked his reflection in the mirror and straightened his tie. He had been expecting the visitor. She was young, slim and tall, with glossy dark hair brushing her shoulders. A vision of delight, and perfect for what he had in mind.

"Come in. You found the place alright, then?" He'd worried about that, not knowing how far she'd have to travel.

She brushed past him and clipped across the parquet floor. The smell of cheap perfume made him want to gag. The man shook his head. High heels. Hardly suitable attire for a cleaner.

In the kitchen, she stood and faced him. "You know the deal. It was all in the ad I placed. A hundred, and I don't stay more than an hour. What do you want me to do first?"

The man licked his lips. Short and to the point. She had a foreign accent that he couldn't quite place. Well, no matter. An hour? Not very long for the money. It didn't bother him, he'd got the girl here under false pretences anyway. Whatever she usually did for her clients, the service he required tonight was of a quite different sort. She wasn't here to clean. She was here to suffer. And finally, when he tired of her, to die.

"I thought you could start in here." He glanced around the kitchen.

"If we must." She turned her back on him, took out an overall from her bag and with a wriggle, pulled it over her slim frame.

In the corner, a rack of shelves. Perched on the middle shelf, and trained on the large, battered kitchen table, sat a small camera. He didn't collect trophies. He preferred to film the proceedings. Later, when it was all over, he would sit with a comforting nip of whiskey and savour every moment, again and again. He wanted nothing more from life than simple pleasures such as these.

She stood waiting, ready to begin.

"The money. I don't do anything until I see hard cash."

She had a good figure under that nylon overall, and the foreign accent was rather sexy. Tonight's encounter held promise.

"Give me a moment." *Quick, don't arouse her suspicions.* He reached into a cupboard behind her and picked out the claw hammer.

One swing to the side of her head. That's all it took. It connected with a sickening crunch, and the girl toppled like a felled pine.

It wasn't hard to manhandle her up onto the table. She was slight, and he was strong. She lay on her back, blood oozing from the head wound. A soft moan escaped her lips and she stirred slightly. Soon she would regain consciousness. He didn't want to hear her screams, not yet. He stuffed her mouth with a dishcloth.

He lifted the bag onto the table and took out its contents, one by one. A mobile, which he switched off. A bag with make-up in it. A purse, containing a fiver in change, and in the inside flap, a photo. A small child, smiling happily at the camera. A little girl no more than two years old, with blonde curls and not a care in the world.

He looked at the camera. Smiled. "She's a mum," he murmured. This was better than he'd expected. A single mother, down on her luck. A young woman who'd do anything to earn a crust. The perfect victim. The child's photo aroused no feelings of tenderness, or anything else. He had a task to complete, and the young woman on the table was simply another tick on his list.

He shook himself. He must get on. The voice in his head wouldn't be still until it got what it wanted.

Do it! Get her to that place you've found, and have some fun.

Chapter 1

Three months later

Henry Johns pointed the gun at the locked door. "Shut it, kid!"

Chloe Addison whimpered. She cowered, hunched in on herself against the wall, with a terrified expression on her young face.

They were holed up in a disused church about half a mile from Leesdon High Street. The place was closed to the public because it was badly in need of repair and deemed to be dangerous. Several ceiling beams had fallen in. Look up, and you could see the sky through the holes where the roofing slates were missing. The stone floor slabs were rutted, strewn with bits of slate and brickwork that had fallen to the ground amongst the litter. It was slippery underfoot, covered in slimy moss. The council had secured the place, or so they thought. The door was solid oak and still intact, and a padlock had been fitted. Job done. But around the back of the church were several gaping holes in the stone wall. The place had become the estate's favourite dump site.

Johns put his eye to the keyhole and squinted through. A crowd had gathered, but he could see only one policeman. "Get lost, copper!" he screamed. "Do one or I'll shoot the girl." Still holding the gun, he grabbed Chloe by her long hair. "Tell them. Tell them I mean it."

But Chloe couldn't speak. She was crying, her teeth chattering and her small form shaking with fear.

Henry turned to her and jerked his head. "Get back there. Find something to barricade this door."

Someone in the crowd outside shouted, "Let the child go, Henry. This has gone far enough."

"This is all your fault! Interfering bastards. I wasn't doing nothing wrong. I went in that shop to ask about booze for Saturday's party. It's my ma's birthday. Bob shouldn't have shouted at me like that."

"Henry, let the girl come outside and we'll talk about it. You're not a bad lad, we know that. You have a short fuse, that's all. Your temper runs away with you."

The policeman banged on the door again. The noise tore at Henry's nerve ends. The crowd shouted and shrieked obscenities, chanting his name. And on top of it all, the kid was wailing her heart out. It was all too much.

Chloe seemed to be trying to tell him something. She tugged at the hem of his hoodie. He batted her away like a fly. The kid was only six years old, her parents would be frantic. He had no idea how he was going to get out of this.

"Why did Bob press that alarm? Why?" Henry screamed at the door. "He knows me, does Bob. He knows damn well I wouldn't hurt anyone."

* * *

PC Phil Seaton had radioed in for backup and an armed response unit. That was over fifteen minutes ago. The crowd was getting ugly, and he was on his own. If they put their minds to it, they could be inside that church within minutes. God help Henry Johns then. Gun or not, they'd bloody lynch him.

"Come on, Henry. The police'll be here any second. They'll have guns, the whole works. It'll go better for you if you come out willingly."

Henry was still shouting. "It's all gone wrong! I didn't mean to snatch the girl! You have to tell 'em. Make it right again. It were them kids, not me. They gave me the gun. They dared me to do it."

"I'll tell them, Henry. Let Chloe come out first, and we'll talk. It'll be better to do it before the others get here." PC Seaton turned to the crowd and tried to usher them back. He'd strung a length of police tape in front of the church, but it was being universally disregarded. "If the girl's gonna stand any chance, you get back and stay quiet," he ordered them sharply.

As a rule, Henry was harmless, but recently he'd been a bundle of nerves. He'd become mixed up with a gang of young lads, the latest bunch of Hobfield troublemakers. They egged him on, dared him to do things he'd ordinarily never even think of. This gun, the trouble in the off license, were a case in point.

At last, Seaton heard the sirens. Three cars tore down the main road and screeched to a halt by the church gates. This was it. Time was up for Henry.

A sergeant strode towards him.

"I think I can get him to come out," PC Seaton called to him. "He knows me. We can't take any risks. He's got a child in there, a little girl. We've been talking. He knows he can't hold out."

But the sergeant didn't look like he wanted to wait. Someone handed him a megaphone and he addressed the church door.

"Open the door now. Toss the gun out first, then come out with your hands up."

The crowd had fallen back at the approach of the police. Silence, not even a whisper. This was no longer the local beat bobby and the estate clown providing free entertainment. This was serious.

A single shot rang out.

Like greyhounds from the starting box, several police officers raced towards the door.

"Chloe!" PC Seaton shouted, his heart thumping. Surely Henry wouldn't be so stupid? "Are you okay?"

The little girl cried out. PC Seaton closed his eyes in relief. "Stand away from the door, Chloe!"

A uniformed officer broke the door down with an enforcer and seconds later, they were in. Henry Johns lay on the ground in a pool of blood, the gun still in his hand.

PC Seaton bent down and felt for a pulse. "He's still alive!"

The ambulance had just arrived, and two paramedics ran in and knelt by Henry. Chloe Addison was shaking, and her dirty face was streaked with tears. PC Seaton scooped her up and carried her outside.

"I was frightened," she sobbed. "Henry didn't hurt me, but the lady looked horrible. I didn't want to stay in there with her."

The lady? The words made no sense. "Is the child okay?" a paramedic asked.

PC Seaton put Chloe on her feet, and looked her up and down. Her clothes were dishevelled and dirty, but she seemed to be unharmed.

She pulled at PC Seaton's arm. "You've gotta look at the lady. She's all black and bony. She's stuck on that beam, and there's nails coming out of her."

The sergeant peered inside and bellowed at his men. "Get forensics down here! Looks like the kid is right."

PC Seaton handed Chloe to the paramedic and went to look for himself. Behind the altar, half-hidden by panelling, the body of a woman was propped up against one of the supporting oak beams. Her hands and feet had been nailed to the wood.

The sergeant grimaced. "Been here a while. The rats have been at her too. Look, her feet are on the floor and they've nibbled her toes."

"How come no one noticed?" PC Seaton asked. "Folk come here a lot. They dump rubbish. There was a homeless bloke dossing down here for a while."

The sergeant shrugged. "She's in the shadows. And that old screen blocks the view from the door."

One of the paramedics was peering over their shoulders. "This didn't happen today. She's been here for a while."

* * *

"Inspector Calladine, are you still here?" DCI Rhona Birch shouted down the corridor.

Tom Calladine winced. "Yes, ma'am," he said, "just getting my stuff together." In fact, he was still ploughing through a load of paperwork for an impending trial. He had hoped to get in another hour at least.

"I told you to go home." She stood in his office doorway, hands on her ample hips. Calladine heard the irritation in her voice.

"You are ill, Calladine. Haven't you seen your face?"

He avoided her gaze. "Well, yes. It *is* a bit of a mess. I'll stick some cream on it when I get home. I'm sure it's nothing serious."

"It's shingles, man! All down one side of your cheek, and it's weeping. You are infectious. Now will you go home before you spread the virus to the rest of the station."

"Sorry. Didn't realise," he muttered. "I'll go now."

"You mustn't come back until it's scabbed over and dried up. Do you understand? A visit to your GP wouldn't go amiss either. He'll give you some antivirals."

Calladine sighed inwardly. "What about my workload? The preparations for the trial? What about Chief Superintendent Ford?"

"As for your workload," Birch said, "your team have nothing urgent on at present. You'll only be off a day or two, and the trial is a week away. Angus Ford is not an issue. His visit will be short and sweet. He'll be based at Oldston, not here. The powers that be might have given him responsibility for this station too, but the reality is, Oldston will take up most of his time."

Something to be grateful for at least. The old chief super from Oldston had moved on. Ford, the new incumbent, would be spread thin with both Oldston and Leesdon to oversee. Calladine didn't relish the prospect. He knew Ford of old, and wondered if he was still the bad-tempered bugger he'd been back then.

"I want you out of here in the next ten minutes." Birch wagged a finger at him, and turned and left him in peace.

It was gone six in the evening and growing dark. The main office was empty apart from Joyce, the admin assistant, who was packing up ready to leave for the day. Rocco and Alice were down in the canteen getting some tea. Ruth had gone with a uniform to an incident at the old church on Brookdale Road. He'd ring her later to find out what it was all about. It was no good fighting against Birch. She wanted him gone and he didn't have the energy to resist. He shoved a pile of paperwork into his briefcase, nodded at Joyce and left without a word. It hurt his jaw to talk.

Shingles! God knows where he'd picked that up, but it was damned painful. A couple of days on the sofa would do him good. He lived an easy walk from the station, and this morning he'd decided to do just that.

Layla, his new girlfriend, was all for the two of them adopting a healthier lifestyle. She was a paramedic, and saw first-hand what junk food and booze did to folk by the time they reached middle age. With any luck she'd have finished her shift and would sort him out with some strong painkillers.

All his life, Calladine had lived in the same Leesdon street. He now lived a few metres from the house he'd been brought up in. The stone-built terraced houses would once have accommodated Leesdon's millworkers, and these days, much to Calladine's surprise, were much sought after. Nestled up against the Pennine hills, Leesdon, part of an area known as Leesworth, was fast becoming a fashionable place to live.

The new woman in his life, Layla, lived across the road. Her irregular hours as a paramedic meant she was able to look after his dog Sam. As he strolled towards his house he heard Sam barking a welcome. But there was no sign of Layla's car. Dammit. She must still be at work.

Calladine felt dreadful. Now he had a headache kicking in. All he wanted was a hot drink, some telly and then bed. His car was parked outside his house. He stood beside it and, fishing in his coat pocket for his house keys, bent and put down his briefcase. As he did so, someone struck the back of his neck. Calladine tried to get up, to defend himself, tackle his assailant. But a stronger blow knocked him to the ground and he fell back, unconscious.

Chapter 2

Day 1

Sergeant Ruth Bayliss was in early the next morning. She and a uniformed PC had attended what was reported as an 'incident' late yesterday afternoon at the church on Brookside Road. Ruth hadn't been told what to expect, and was totally unprepared for the horror that confronted her. A woman, who'd been dead for some time, left naked and nailed to one of the old beams in the church. In the absence of DI Calladine, it was down to her to brief the team. She'd bring him up to speed as soon as he turned up.

DC Simon Rockliffe, known as Rocco, DC Alice Bolshaw, a couple of uniformed officers and Joyce gathered around the incident board.

"A young woman," Ruth began, "dead for some time. Exactly how she died has yet to be established. What I can tell you is that she'd had her throat slit. She was left nailed to a supporting beam at the back of the church."

"Murdered, then," Rocco interrupted.

Ruth frowned at him. "Very much so. Dr Barrington will do the PM this morning."

"Do we have an ID?" Alice asked.

"Not yet, Alice. There was nothing left with her that might help. Unless CSI find something, all I know is what I saw. A young woman, long dark hair, skinny, and very dead."

"Dumped, then," Rocco said.

"Dumped suggests it was done quickly. Whoever put her there wasn't in any hurry. It must have been hard to get her up that high. The CSI officers will do a thorough search. If the killer left anything behind, they'll find it. The post-mortem will be a tough one. The wound I saw, the nails driven through the hands and feet, suggest she didn't have an easy death. Dr Barrington will have some harrowing details for us." She looked at Rocco. "You can come with me."

The office door opened. "DI Calladine will not be in for a day or two," announced DCI Birch. "He's ill. Can you manage?"

"Yes, ma'am. I'm sure we'll cope for a couple of days while he's off. I'm just briefing the team on the Brookside Road murder." Ruth smiled at her.

"Okay, but remember, in Calladine's absence I'm available to help. Though I do have several meetings arranged for this week. One of them is an event in Oldston that'll take a full day. I'll brief DI Long, and DS Thorpe can give you a hand if necessary. They have nothing much on at the moment. I read the initial report. It's a bad one. You must ask for help if you get nowhere within the next twenty-four hours." Birch turned and left.

"What's up with him?" Ruth asked.

"He had a nasty rash all down one side of his face," Joyce said. "Shingles, according to the DCI. It came up suddenly yesterday afternoon. He looked a right mess, so she sent him home. I'm surprised he didn't ring you."

So was Ruth. He was her DI, but they were close friends too. He could have let her know. "Sent home by the boss. I bet he loved that. I'm sorry for him, really I am, but he's landed us with Long. And even worse, Thorpe." She rolled her eyes. "I know it's a big ask, but let's try and sort this one quickly if we can. It'll save us a load of hassle."

They all nodded. None of them relished the prospect of having Long and Thorpe in their midst.

"And if we can't, let's hope the boss gets back quickly," Rocco added.

"Has your little Harry had chickenpox?" Joyce asked.

Ruth shook her head. "He's had nothing much. A few sniffles so far, that's all."

"In that case I'd keep him away from the boss. I've an idea you can catch one from the other," Joyce said.

"Come to think about it, I've never had chickenpox myself. That means I'd better give him a miss too. If I get it, Harry's bound to pick it up."

Rocco was grinning. "He won't like missing this. Juicy murder, unknown female. Just the sort of stuff we can really get stuck into."

"It's not a game, Rocco," Ruth said sharply. Rocco hadn't attended the crime scene. Well, she had, and it would be a while before she got the image out of her head. "The poor woman is dead. Killed horribly. Her family and friends'll be missing her. They need to know what happened. We need an ID on her as soon as. That can be your job, Alice. Trawl through missing persons. See what turns up."

"You think she was local?" Alice asked.

Ruth shrugged. "Who knows? With luck, Dr Barrington will give us something we can work with. If she does, I'll let you know straight away. In the meantime, see what you can find, Alice. You're good at that stuff."

Indeed, she was. Alice Bolshaw had helped them with a case long before she became a detective. She was meticulous and seemed to enjoy the small details of an investigation. When she'd first joined them, Alice had been a geeky student, far too serious for one so young. These days she was more relaxed, but she still applied the same rigour to her work. Alice had even taken it upon herself to look back at past cases the various units at the station had dealt with. Ruth was aware that she'd asked to see Calladine about a couple of them.

"Will you speak to the boss later?" Rocco asked.

"I'll ring him. See how he is. Let him know we're coping."

"He'll want to know about the new case," Rocco said.

Ruth smiled. "And I'll tell him. But it won't hurt him to wait a few hours."

Chapter 3

"How many times have we stood here?" Ruth said.

She and Rocco were on the low parapet overlooking the business end of the post-mortem room.

"Too many times." Rocco nodded at the body Natasha Barrington's assistant had just uncovered. "And it doesn't get any easier. Look at her. That is some mess. Who does that to another human being?"

"A monster, DC Rockliffe," Natasha called up. "So we'd better get our heads together and catch him soon."

The sight of the body was getting to Ruth, but the smell was not too bad. "Why is decomposition not more advanced?"

"It's been a cold winter," Natasha said. "That old church has no heating and part of it's open to the elements. There'll have been times when the body literally froze. Two weeks ago, for example. One night it was six below."

"Lucky for us," Rocco whispered. "It could help with identification."

Natasha indicated to various places on the body. "It was murder. Pretty obvious, I suppose. She suffered a blow to the head, something wooden. There are tiny splinters in the wound."

"Like a baseball bat?" Rocco asked.

"No, something smaller. But it had a smooth edge. The blow left a nasty cut and a large bruise, but it didn't fracture her skull. It bled into her hair, but that wasn't what killed her. Her throat was slit, from ear to ear. However, prior to that the killer inflicted a number of other wounds. He then nailed her by the hands and feet to the beam in the church. The wounds bled. CSI are checking the beam for blood."

"You think that's where he killed her?" Ruth asked.

"Forensic analysis of the area will tell us for sure, but I would say so. He also branded her. See the mark across her midriff? It looks like a sideways on letter 'T.' Natasha paused, her mouth a thin line. "You've got a bad one here. He spared her nothing. Apart from the head wound and the burn, there are numerous puncture wounds in the flesh of her arms and legs. There wasn't much meat on her. It's hard to tell because of the state of the body, but she wouldn't have put up much of a fight. She'd have been semi-conscious, unable to defend herself. It would have made his task simple." Natasha stepped back for a moment. "We'll do all the usual tests. See if she was drugged. I hope for her sake, she was."

Ruth watched Natasha make the necessary incisions preparatory to opening the body. She felt sick.

"The contents have deteriorated, but there is undigested meat in her stomach, cut into small chunks. Stew perhaps?"

The poor woman had eaten just before meeting her killer. "DNA?" Ruth asked.

"There's a good chance," Natasha said.

"We are hoping to get an identity pretty quick," Ruth was looking away, "but we need a lead on her killer."

"CSI are still going over the site where she was found. But I'm told that that old church is in a helluva mess. They might find the tools the killer used — discarded nails, the wooden implement used to cosh her over the head. But the search will take time."

Ruth felt lightheaded, and took several deep breaths. This was far worse than she'd thought. They were up against a monster. She tried to imagine the pain this woman must have felt. What must have gone through her mind during the ghastly experience? The plight of this young woman moved her deeply. Ruth was a professional, used to death, but now she was close to tears.

Natasha was speaking again. "It's difficult to tell exactly what she would have looked like. Her mouth has been mutilated. There are teeth missing. Her tongue and the area at the back of her throat have been burnt too, perhaps an attempt to hamper identification via dental records. But she had long dark hair, if that helps."

They watched while Natasha examined the hair more closely. "It was cut recently, but not very well. The ends are uneven. Still, the local hairdressers may give you something."

"Can you give us anything to help identify her?" Ruth asked.

Natasha looked doubtful. "I'll do my best, but it won't be easy. She was found naked, and there's no jewellery or handbag. I'll put photos on the system. What I can do is get one of our forensic artists to do a mock-up of what her face might have looked like. And we'll do further tests. Provided it's on record, the DNA will give you her name. Failing that, I'll try fingerprints, but I can't promise due to the extent of decomposition. I would say she's been dead roughly three months."

Natasha was looking through the girl's hair again, at the back of her scalp and neck. "There's something here." She picked up a magnifying glass. "She has a mark just below the nape of her neck. Her long hair covers it up, but if she wore it short, it would show. It's a birthmark, or perhaps a tattoo, the state of the body makes it difficult to make out. I'll have a closer look, do some tests, and let you know."

"Can you give us anything on her age?" Ruth asked.

"Young. I'd say early twenties. And she's given birth."

That might be useful, but it wasn't much. A couple of crumbs to take back to the waiting flock. Ruth had been hoping for more.

* * *

Ruth and Rocco made their way back to the carpark in silence. Ruth was edgy. She was disappointed at the lack of any positive ID. Taking on this case in Calladine's absence was a big deal professionally. She wanted to do well for personal reasons too. Jake Ireson, her partner, was still considering an offer he'd had from a private school in the south of England. For a teacher at a Leesworth comprehensive, it was very tempting. For starters, it meant more money and better prospects. The final decision was still to be made, but Ruth wanted to stay put. She'd made a pact with herself. If Jake agreed to stay in Leesdon, then she'd put in for DI. A big step, but it would take some of the financial pressure off Jake.

Rocco broke the silence. "Three months dead, and a mum. It's a start, I suppose."

Being the mum of a toddler herself, this worried Ruth. "Why has no one come forward, Rocco? There's a kid out there without its mother. You'd think someone would have noticed! I for one want to know who's caring for the child."

"Alice might find something. She's good at working with the difficult stuff."

"How are you two doing?" Ruth asked.

Rocco and Alice had been in a relationship for a few weeks. The team were surprised when they found out, because they had such different personalities.

"Not that good, if I'm honest. We started off fine, but I think she's gone off me. I ask her out and she comes up with an excuse. Well, I'm a big lad. I can take a hint."

"You could be misreading the signals," Ruth said.

He shook his head. "Don't think so. They seem plain enough to me."

"Is there anyone else on the scene do you think?"

"Who knows?" Rocco shrugged. "She's good at keeping the personal stuff to herself, is Alice."

But Ruth's mind was back on the case. "The little girl Henry held captive. She saw the body. It might be worth talking to her. Ask if she touched or saw anything. You never know."

Chapter 4

Alenka Plesec froze on the spot. Danny Newton, known as 'Newt,' was talking to a group of kids at the entrance to Heron House, one of the tower blocks on the Hobfield estate. He was one to avoid, particularly if you owed him money. Alenka would have doubled back and hidden until he'd gone. But with a child in a pushchair, that was out of the question. Alenka's heart sank. He'd seen her.

"Alenka, babe! I was about to pay you a call. I've come to collect," Newt said.

Just what she didn't want. Newt on her back. For the last couple of weeks, she'd been delivering his dodgy drugs to various customers around the estate. They paid her in cash. Cash that Alenka should have passed on to Newt. But she hadn't done that. All the money she'd collected had gone on rent for the flat, and on stuff for her child.

She tried to push past him. "Can't stop. Lara needs feeding."

Alenka was slender, with long dark hair flowing over her shoulders. Seriously underdressed for the chilly March weather, she wore a cropped top that exposed her midriff, skinny jeans slashed at the knees and a puffer jacket.

Alenka was pretty, but wore too much make-up. Her eyes were ringed with dark kohl, stern beneath thick brows.

He glared at her. "You sold the stuff. You got paid. Fair enough, to take your cut, but you owe me." He leaned closer and grabbed hold of her arm. "People don't cheat me, babe. It makes me angry."

She wasn't strong enough to wriggle free, and it was unlikely that anyone would help her. People round here were too afraid of Newt. "I didn't cheat you. Not on purpose. I needed that money or we'd have had nowhere to live. Give me a bit more time, Newt. I'll find it."

"That was valuable gear. You collected hundreds. The money you got, I have to pass on. What do I tell the big boss now? I know what. Perhaps I should make *you* explain." He laughed.

"Please don't do that, Newt. I'll get it! Tell your boss I'll pay as soon as I can."

He leaned forward and whispered in her ear. "You've given the both of us one huge problem. The boss'll have me beaten to a pulp if I tell him this little tale. He'll come after you too. Piss him off, like you have me, and you're dead meat. Not sure what to tell him now. Mention your name and, kid or not, you won't last the week."

"Give me a chance, Newt. Please. I have to look after Lara. I will help, I'll find the money somehow. You can't tell anyone what I did."

"Come back to work then. You're a natural. You wander round this estate with that pram and no one takes a blind bit of notice. I've got some prime stuff to sell. A whole new supply. It's cheap too. It'd get you out of trouble."

"Heroin?" She wasn't going to touch that.

"Nah. Meth, spice and other stuff. I can get an unlimited supply. We'll clean up. No other firm'll be able to match our prices."

"I don't like having the stuff around the kid."

He laughed. "Do as you're told. She's the perfect cover. Use her. You and I both know that your little flirtation with motherhood could come unstuck at any time. Other folk might not have put it together, but I know the truth."

"Leave me alone! Say anything about me and I'll go to the police. I'll tell them all about the dealing. I saw what you were doing with those kids. You were selling dope."

He grabbed the neck of her jacket. "Do that and you'll suffer."

She stared him down. Newt had the gaunt half-starved look of an addict. His clothes were scruffy and his hair hadn't seen a barber in years. "Just leave it be," she said. "Don't fuck with my life and I'll stay out of yours."

"And the money?"

"I'll find a way."

"Shame, babe. You used to be such a laugh. You and Ingrid."

"Get lost, Newt. Leave me alone."

"Can't do that. Want what's owed. I'm not a charity, and neither is the boss Change your mind and you know where I am."

Alenka had been lucky to get away. Newt had a temper. But more importantly, he could get her into real trouble. He really did know the truth about her 'flirtation with motherhood,' as he put it. If he chose to, he could change her life drastically. Three months ago, her sister Ingrid had asked her to babysit for a couple of hours one evening while she was at work. Alenka wasn't doing anything else, loved her little niece, and had been happy to agree. Ingrid had gone out at about seven.

When they both moved to the estate, Ingrid worked for Newt too. But they'd argued and she told him she'd had enough. Ingrid had her faults, but she was ambitious and hardworking. She'd made a decision to do cleaning work while she waited for something better to turn up. She put ads in the local paper and in shop windows. That evening, she'd received a call and gone out to work.

She'd never returned.

The normal reaction would have been to go to the police. But Alenka had thought better of it. She didn't want the attention. There was the business with Newt. The police would have asked questions that Alenka couldn't answer. Besides, Alenka believed that her sister had done a runner. Ingrid hated the flat, and she hated being a mother. She'd freely admitted that baby Lara cramped her style. Ingrid was selfish. She didn't look after Lara properly and had left her alone on numerous occasions. It salved Alenka's conscience to believe that Ingrid had spotted her chance and grabbed it. Any other possibility she swept from her mind.

Taking Ingrid's place was easy. Both were young, with long dark hair. They were Slovenian, spoke alike, looked alike, and kept themselves to themselves. People in the block mostly ignored them and when they did chat, often got them mixed up. The girls were close, and they shared a flat. The result was that it had been easy for Alenka to take on Ingrid's roles, and so far, no one had challenged her.

Alenka did lie awake some nights wondering what had happened to her sister. She did love Ingrid. Alenka firmly believed that one day she'd come back. She'd have money and take them all away from this dump of an estate.

It did mean that Alenka now had to care for Ingrid's daughter, her niece. But it was no hardship. Lara was an angel, a joy to have in her life. The child was only eighteen months old and wouldn't remember anything of this time. With Alenka looking after her, Lara was content. She thrived.

The only person who had the power to put an end to her new life was Newt. He wasn't stupid. Given half a chance, he would use the fact of Ingrid's disappearance against her. Alenka's one wish was to be rid of him.

Chapter 5

Tom Calladine's eyes snapped open. Something had woken him, but it wasn't a noise. The bedroom was as silent as the grave. It could only have been the strong sunlight streaming in through the window and striking his face.

It took a few seconds for him to recall what had happened. Ah yes. Someone had hit him. Calladine touched the back of his head. He could feel a small lump, and it ached a little. He presumed he'd been the victim of a robbery and was annoyed that he hadn't got a look at his attacker.

Calladine raised himself onto his elbows. He was lying on a double bed in an unfamiliar room. Hospital? Had the knock on the head been that serious? But this didn't look like a hospital room. It was full of old-fashioned furniture. The wallpaper looked ancient. Several paintings were dotted about, all suspended on chains from an oak picture rail. Who had brought him here, and why?

Calladine sat up slowly. The movement made his headache worse. He swung his legs over the edge of the bed and tried to stand. The room swam, and he fell backwards again. This was more than a knock on the head. He'd been drugged too. He closed his eyes. He had to concentrate, try and remember exactly what had happened.

He'd been outside his house, just about to go in. He had no idea how long ago that was. He turned slightly. A digital clock on the bedside table told him only that it was three p.m. But what day?

"Tom!" A woman spoke from the doorway. "You had me worried. I thought you were never going to surface."

Calladine sat up, leaning on the pillows for support. The woman wasn't younger than him. Maybe in her mid-forties? She was slim with short dark hair. Calladine immediately noticed her large, bright blue eyes. She was carrying a tray with tea and toast on it.

"A little something to eat. There are a couple of painkillers too. You have a nasty rash on your face. It looks like shingles to me."

Calladine's hand went to his cheek. Shingles. That was what had taken him home from work.

"Where am I?" he asked.

"You're quite safe. Eat some food and you'll feel stronger."

"Where is this place? Is it a hospital?"

She laughed. "No. It's just a huge old house. It's rather lovely really. It's Victorian, set in glorious countryside."

This failed to impress Calladine. "Why have I been brought here?"

She sighed heavily. "I'm afraid I can't answer that."

"Try harder. You must know where we are."

"You're persistent, aren't you?"

"I'm a policeman. I ask questions. So I'll ask again, where am I?"

"A long way from where you were," she said. "It was thought necessary to keep you out of the way for a while."

"Why?"

"I have no idea. I simply run this house and look after those who are brought here. Don't look to me for answers to your questions, Tom Calladine."

He suddenly realised he was wearing pyjamas. "Where are my things?"

"Your clothes are in that wardrobe. The items you had with you when you were . . . apprehended will be sent back to you in a few days' time."

"Apprehended! I was bloody well attacked and kidnapped. I want my stuff, and then I'm leaving." He was beginning to shout.

"You cannot do that. You must stay here for a while. My advice to you is to make yourself comfortable."

"I'm a prisoner then?"

She inclined her head. "I prefer to think of you as a guest."

"Get me my stuff and then I'm off."

"None of your things are here. They'll be sent to your home once you return." She smiled. "You can get dressed and come downstairs, but you cannot leave the house. I suggest you have some breakfast first. It's a while since you've eaten anything." The woman set the tray down on the table beside him and left.

What was going on? He'd been knocked unconscious, drugged, and brought to this strange place against his will. But why? Well, he certainly had no intention of staying. Energised by anger, he struggled to his feet and shuffled to the window. The woman was right. The countryside was glorious. His heart sank. The view contained nothing but green fields and distant mountains. No buildings of any kind. There were no roads either, just a narrow track up to the house.

This had to be the work of a person with a score to settle. Someone had got him out of the way to serve a purpose. The only thing Calladine could think of was the Costello trial. He was scheduled to give evidence next week. But it didn't make sense. His testimony alone wouldn't send the villain down. The CPS had much more on Costello.

Calladine searched through the chest of drawers next to the bed. Nothing. He looked in the wardrobe. His clothes were there, as she'd said, but there was no mobile or wallet. He couldn't contact anyone, couldn't tell a soul what had happened to him. They'd be thinking all sorts. Did they know he'd been kidnapped? He'd gone home sick. Were they even looking for him? It was a sobering thought.

Chapter 6

They left the morgue and Rocco drove them back to the nick. Earlier that day, Ruth had believed she could do this. He might be one of her closest friends and she was sorry he was sick, but Calladine's absence had given her an opportunity to prove herself. It was a chance to show the powers that be that she could step up. But the post-mortem had upset her. Now, after what she'd seen during the last hour, her emotions threatened to get in the way. Her next task was to brief the team, but she was doubting her ability to even do that without dissolving into tears. She'd seen a lot of sick crimes during her time at Leesdon station, but this was certainly up there with the worst.

"We've got a right nutter on our hands," Rocco muttered.

"Please, that doesn't help. The poor girl. It doesn't bear thinking about." Ruth closed her eyes. The image of what she'd seen in the church, coupled with the sight in the PM room made her heave. What sort of sicko does all that stuff to a young woman?

"Problem is, Ruth, we *have* to think about it. We have to think quick too. Who knows when he'll strike again?" Rocco said.

"She's been dead a while," she said, clutching at straws. "We haven't found another body."

"We wouldn't have found this one for a while if not for that incident with Henry Johns. There could be others. We just don't know. This wasn't a spur of the moment murder, Ruth. He took his time, probably even planned it. We could be looking for a serial killer. If so, there'll be more."

Ruth heaved a sigh. She didn't want to hear it, but Rocco was right. "I might give Tom a ring later."

"Ask his advice?" Rocco smirked.

"Tom does have more experience than me. He won't mind. He'll be missing the cut and thrust of the job anyway. It'll give him something to think about while he recovers. When he does come back, he won't thank me if I keep him in the dark. Once he knows what we're dealing with, he'll want in, mark my words."

"You could speak to Birch," Rocco said.

"Uh-uh. Only if I have to. Tom seems to rub along with her okay, but she terrifies me! Anyway, Birch will only assign Long to the job."

"She'll read the reports as they come in. Birch'll know what we're up against. Don't be surprised if she puts the entire nick onto it."

Ruth groaned. "Why did Tom have to go and get sick now? He's never ill."

* * *

Back at the nick, Ruth assembled the team. She pointed to the notes from the PM that she'd written on the board. "This is a bad one. We need a lot more information. We need the victim's life up there for a start. Make it a priority. For now, all we know is that she's young, and has had a child. Alice, did you find anything?"

"No one in their early twenties has been reported missing during the last six months. Prior to that, it was kids mostly, simple runaways. And they've all turned up safe."

"Our victim could be from out of the area," Rocco said. "It might be worth a shot to extend the scope of the search."

"This is Greater Manchester we're talking about. Leesworth might not have any missing people, but the area as a whole has plenty. Hundreds, in fact." Ruth nodded at Alice. "Carry on looking. Natasha'll let us know if her DNA is on record as soon as she can."

"Ruth!" DCI Rhona Birch beckoned Ruth out into the corridor. "How did it go?"

"We're waiting on the results of tests, ma'am. There was nothing on the body to immediately identify her. In the meantime, we're looking at missing persons. The woman had given birth, so there is a child somewhere. It seems odd that no one has reported her missing."

"If our victim was very young, perhaps the child was given up for adoption, taken into care," Birch suggested.

She had a point. "We'll look into it. Check if Social Services have any record."

"Have you heard from Calladine?" Birch asked.

"No. I thought I'd ring him tonight. Tell him what we're up to."

"If you speak to him, let me know, will you? This case looks like it's going to be big. I might assign DI Long's team to it. Pull out all the stops. You can be sure the new chief super will be monitoring progress."

Birch headed back to her office.

Ruth groaned. Long! Just what she needed.

When Ruth returned to the team, Alice told her that Doctor Barrington had been on the phone. "She'd like a word."

"I'll ring her in a minute." She faced them — Rocco, Alice, and Joyce, the admin assistant. Not many. With

Calladine absent they were a body down. They'd be pushed. "Birch will give the case to Long if we don't get something soon. I don't want that. There's a new chief super on our tails too."

"That'll be Angus Ford," Joyce said. "He's got responsibility for Oldston and us now."

"Does that mean Edwin Walker's retired?" Ruth asked.

Joyce nodded.

Ruth was aware that the old chief super was Eve Buckley's brother. Eve was Calladine's birth mother.

Rocco looked around at the others. "We don't want any of that either, do we? The longer the new incumbent stays away, the better."

The other two mumbled in assent.

"It's in our own interest to crack on," Ruth said. "We give it everything — not that we don't anyway. Our victim had given birth, Alice. There is a child out there missing its mother. Someone must be looking after the kid. Perhaps a relative. I don't understand why they haven't come forward, banged on our door long and hard."

Point made, Ruth used the office phone to call Natasha.

"Given that we have very little, I thought you should know right away," Natasha said. "I've had another look at the mark on her neck. It's a birthmark. Our victim had a tattooed outline drawn around it at some time, made it larger and more heart-shaped. I've put a photo on the system for you."

It was something. "We'll look into it. Thank you."

"Julian is going to call in and see you. He's been back and forth to the crime scene and he wants to talk to you urgently."

"Did he say why?" Ruth asked.

"No, but it must be important. You know Julian."

Ruth put the receiver down. "Tattoo parlours," she announced. "The victim had a birthmark enhanced.

Rocco, get the photo off the system and try the local places. It's a little different, so with luck, someone might remember it."

Chapter 7

Alice pinned the crime scene photos to the board. "These are grim," she said.

"The reality was worse, believe me," Ruth murmured, looking closer. Although she had attended the scene, it had been dark, and the old church was dangerous, so access had been restricted. Plus, there was junk strewn everywhere. The CSI officers would have a problem deciding what was relevant and what wasn't. Even so, the sight was dreadful, and the smell of decaying rubbish even worse. After a quick look round, Ruth had been grateful to leave it to scenes of crime.

"I read about something like this recently," Alice said.

"What do you mean?" Ruth asked her.

"I've been looking at old case notes," she explained. "You might think that a bit odd but I have so little hands-on experience, it helps me to understand the work we do. I've been studying DI Calladine's old cases in particular."

Thinking back to the Alice they first knew back in her uni days this was typical behaviour Ruth realised.

"There was one murder like this one — victim branded, throat slit, nailed to a tree and left with no identification. Before he went off sick I asked the inspector what cases he recommended and this was among the ones he noted down."

"Find me the details, Alice. They could be important."

"I'll get my notes. They're on my desk."

Ruth peered more closely at the photos. She couldn't recall a case like this one, but Calladine obviously did. As Alice had pointed out, he had worked it.

A minute later, Alice stood behind her, file in hand. "He was nicknamed the 'teddy bear butcher.' They found a soft toy he'd left at the scene."

"Like this?" Ruth pointed to one of the photos. A pink teddy bear was lying discarded on the floor, easily missed in among the detritus strewn about. "Does that fit the description?"

Alice nodded. "Possibly. I noticed it too, but the floor of the church is covered in rubbish, so we shouldn't jump to conclusions. However, given what I read in this file, I took the liberty of asking the CSI officers to take a look at that soft toy."

"Good. You did well." Typical Alice. "Who investigated the original killing?"

Alice looked at the file. "According to this, DI Calladine, he was still a DS back then. Another one was DS Angus Ford."

Ruth realised that this was the new chief superintendent.

"The investigation was run from Oldston station. The victim was from that area."

"Who was the SIO?" Ruth asked.

Alice turned a page. "A DCI Boyd, now retired. Another of the team was a DC Andrews. He must have left the force because I can't find any record of him."

Angus Ford. Calladine had spoken about his time with him. He gave her the impression that he disliked the man, although he'd never said why.

"What are you thinking?" Alice asked.

"That we won't jump to conclusions."

"Good advice," Rocco said from his desk. "This is a bad day. We should wait and see what scenes of crime throw into the pot before we let panic set in."

But the image of the teddy bear remained in her mind. She checked the dates in the file. The case Alice had drawn her attention to was twenty years old. It must have been one of the last cases Tom had worked on before being made up to DI. The file stated that a woman had been killed in a very similar way to their current victim. She was also found nailed up and branded. A small teddy was left near the body with the stuffing replaced with the victim's hair. This was more than just coincidence. She'd have to wait and see what CSI found.

There was a knock on the incident room door. "DS Bayliss?"

Ruth turned and stared at the stranger. He was about her own age, tall, dressed in jeans, a T-shirt and a casual jacket. Long, tousled fair hair framed his face. It suited him. He had an infectious smile and a twinkle in his eyes. The unexpected sight of this man sent a little shiver down Ruth's spine. Not like her. What was going on?

She smiled. "That's me."

"I'm Michael Turner, the forensic artist attached to the Duggan. Dr Barrington asked me to speak to you."

"You're here about our victim?"

He nodded, frowning. "Unfortunately, yes. I'll help if I can. My job is to attempt a facial likeness."

"Have you seen the victim? You do know what you're dealing with?" Ruth was dubious.

"I'm not squeamish. This is what I do. I've seen it all during my time in forensics. This case is difficult because of the damage done to her mouth and the extent of decomposition, so any likeness will be approximate. But the shape of the head, the forehead, cheek bones and jawline will give me most of what I need. I'll prepare several likenesses with different mouth shapes."

That sounded fine. Who could tell? If the girl was local, it might be enough. "How long will it take you?"

His accent was slightly northern. "Just a few days. I'll ring you in the morning and arrange a meeting for later in the week. You'll be able to use the images in the media. Hopefully someone'll recognise her."

"I've not seen you before. Been at the Duggan long?" Ruth asked.

"No, I used to be attached to Chesterfield police. You know — the town with the bent church spire?" He smiled.

"Is that where you come from?" She was being nosey now.

He didn't seem offended. "Yes. My parents are still there. But if you want to get on, you have to spread your wings. The Duggan is a centre of excellence. A spell there and I reckon someone like me could get a position anywhere."

Ruth inclined her head. "Ambitious."

"I've no ties, so why not?"

Ruth smiled. Why did the knowledge that he was unattached please her? She was being stupid. It must be the stress of the case. Since the day she'd first set eyes on Jake Ireson, Ruth hadn't looked at another man. But by the way this one was affecting her, something had obviously changed.

"You must be ambitious too, surely? The trick is not to get stuck in a rut. You work in policing. It's not a comfortable option, so you might as well get what you can from it."

Michael Turner had a point. Ruth knew she had the experience to make DI. But could she run her own team? And what difference would it make to her relationship with Tom Calladine? She had felt for some time now that she was far too comfortable. Stuck in a rut.

She smiled at him. "For now, I have a murder to solve. I'll think about my future once we've wrapped this one up. Look forward to seeing what you come up with."

"I'll be in touch." He smiled again and left the office.

Straight away, Rocco was on her case. "I saw your face. That bloke touched a nerve, didn't he? You do fancy moving up the ladder. Having to take control while the boss is away, it's given you a taste for it."

"What if it has? You don't intend to stay a DC all your life, do you? You're good, Rocco. You should think about it."

"I do, but for the time being, this nick and the team suit me fine."

Now Ruth felt guilty. He probably thought she was being disloyal. "I'd like to feel like that, but you don't have the same pressures as I do."

"What pressures?"

"A child, an ambitious partner who's been offered a post elsewhere. It takes some dealing with, believe me."

"Where is this post? Not far, I hope?" Rocco looked concerned.

"Some posh school down south," she said. "Jake wants us to move. It would mean a complete change for both of us. He's keen, but I'm out of my depth. I've tried talking to him, but he's not for changing his mind."

"You're not seriously considering it, the pair of you? The boss won't cope without you."

She shrugged. "He might have to."

Now Rocco looked really worried. "You can't leave. The team won't be the same without you."

"Don't underestimate yourself, or the others," Ruth said. "You're good. Alice is more than promising. You'd all do just fine."

Rocco's smile had now become a cheeky grin. "There was something else, something between Turner and you. What do they call it? A *frisson*, that's it. You liked him."

"Rubbish! There is no room for another man in my life right now, even if I wanted one. Which I don't." Ruth felt her face grow hot. She was behaving like a bloody teenager!

"It'd solve the problem of the move though."

Ruth opened her mouth to reply just as Julian came into the room. He looked worried. Professor Julian Batho was the Duggan's senior forensic scientist. Up until her untimely death at the hands of a killer, he and DC Imogen Goode, another member of Calladine's team, had been partners. Recently, Julian had appeared to be finally recovering from his grief. Today, however, his face was drawn, as if he hadn't slept.

"We need to talk," Julian said. "Is Tom around?"

"He's ill, Julian. Birch sent him home yesterday. He's got shingles. If we need his input, I can always ring him."

"We will need him."

Ruth stared at him. "What's happened?"

"After Alice called, I went down to the crime scene. I looked around, took samples. I also checked the record for the case she told me about." Julian walked across to the incident board. "You've seen this." He tapped the photo of the debris strewn across the floor. "At first I thought it was just more rubbish left by fly-tippers. But I was wrong."

Ruth caught her breath. So Alice was right. "It can't be! I've just been looking at the file. That case was wound up. The killer was put away."

The look on Julian's face told her otherwise. "A soft toy, the stuffing ripped out of it and refilled with the victim's hair. It's also smeared with her blood. There is no doubt. It's George Norbury's trademark."

Ruth stared at him. "You and I both know that can't be. Norbury's locked up, has been for years. Tom worked the case. He helped to put him away."

"Nonetheless, the MO is his. The toy, the branding, the slit throat. Nailing the victim to something made of wood." Julian tapped the photo again.

"Copycat?" Rocco suggested.

Julian shook his head.

"Professor Batho is right," Alice said. "In the end, Norbury confessed. From the transcript I read, it would seem he was only too happy to do so. He gave the impression that he was proud of what he'd done. Although the press reported on it, certain details were never released. No protracted trial, you see. One of those details was the soft toy and hair thing. Only a handful of people knew about that. But he always left a toy, usually placed in the victim's hand. The only difference in this case is that it was on the floor."

"The body's been there a while," Ruth said. "The wildlife will have got at it. That toy could well have been moved."

"Natasha tells me the victim's hair had been cut," Julian said.

Ruth nodded. "And he saw her off by slitting her throat. Too many similarities. I don't think this is coincidence."

"We need to speak to Tom urgently," Julian said.

Ruth went to the phone. "I'll ring him now."

Chapter 8

Day 2

Ruth was up and ready to leave by seven thirty the next morning. "You're going into work early," Jake said from beneath the bedclothes.

"Sorry, Jake, heavy day ahead. No Tom and a difficult case. Julian was desperate to speak to him yesterday, but Tom wasn't answering his phone."

"Guessed as much. You were tossing and turning all night, and mumbling in your sleep."

"I rang him half a dozen times yesterday. I can't understand what he's up to."

Jake sat up. "More than likely he took a shedload of painkillers and got to bed early."

"Shingles or not, I'm calling round at his before I go into work."

"Don't get too close," Jake said.

"You'll have to see to Harry and get him to nursery. Okay with that?"

Jake ignored this. "Don't forget, I have to make my decision about the job by the end of this week."

Ruth sighed. "Not now. I can't think of anything but this case. We'll talk later."

"You're getting bogged down again. You and I need to consider what is really important."

That was all very well, but what about her job? That was important too. Until Jake had come along, it had been her whole life. Why didn't he see that? Jake wasn't a selfish person, but he was hell bent on dragging them all down south.

Ruth drove the half mile or so to Calladine's house. The backstreet where he lived was quiet. No through traffic roared to and fro. Everything looked as usual. His car was parked in front of the house and the curtains were open. That should mean he was up and about.

"Ruth!" A woman was calling to her from a doorway opposite.

It was Layla, standing with her dressing gown pulled tight around her. "What have you done with him?"

"He's ill," Ruth called back.

Layla beckoned her over. "He's not there. The place is exactly as he left it two days ago. Even the breakfast dishes are still in the sink. I've got Sam with me. Poor love was starving."

That wasn't right. Was he so ill that he'd had to go and stay with Zoe, his daughter, or even his mother, Eve? But wouldn't he have told Layla? "Have you checked with Zoe?" Ruth said.

"I rang her. She hasn't seen him in over a week. He's not with Eve either."

Ruth needed to get into the house. "In that case, I've no idea what's going on. Do you have a key?"

Layla darted back inside and returned with it. "I thought he must be away on some case. But he always rings me, so I couldn't understand it. I've tried ringing his mobile, but it's dead."

Ruth's stomach turned over. She'd no idea what this meant, but it didn't sound good. Where was he? Why hadn't he got in touch? Ruth let herself into Calladine's house, picking the mail off the mat and depositing it on his hall table. It was March and still chilly, and the place was cold. The heating hadn't been on for some time.

"Tom!" Ruth began to mount the stairs, her nerves jangling. "I'm coming up." Something was terribly wrong.

Layla came up behind her. "I've had a good look round already. He isn't here."

"Our DCI sent him home to rest. He walked that day. I remember making fun of him. He had an apple and an orange for his lunch too."

Layla smiled. "The healthy lifestyle we're trying out."

"His car is still parked outside." Ruth pushed past her and went outside to take a look. It appeared to be okay. She tried the doors. They were locked. "This hasn't moved. Everything is as he would have left it that morning to come to work."

"Have you seen this?" Layla pointed to the front, just below the headlight on the near side. "If I'm not mistaken, that's blood."

Ruth looked at it. Layla was right. The patch was quite large. Fortunately, it hadn't rained in over a week and it had dried on the paintwork. Ruth bent down and peered under the car. Several centimetres in and hidden from view lay a mobile phone. Taking an evidence bag from her pocket, she picked it up. "This is Tom's."

Layla's voice shook. "What's happened? He's been attacked, hasn't he?"

Ruth touched her arm. "Best not jump to conclusions." But she knew that something serious had happened here. Tom had been injured. During the scuffle he'd dropped his phone and it had slid under the car.

"Don't touch anything, Layla," Ruth said. "I'm going to get a forensic team down here."

* * *

"I think Calladine has been attacked and kidnapped, ma'am," Ruth said.

Birch looked sceptical.

"He left here, as you instructed. But he only made it as far as the front of his house. He never went inside. There's blood on his car and I found his mobile phone underneath it." Ruth held up the evidence bag. "We should investigate. I want forensics to take a look."

"And they will," Birch said. "We'll do all we can to find him."

But the words sounded hollow. Birch was holding something back. If the something was about Tom, then Ruth wanted to know. "Do you know anything about this that we don't, ma'am? I for one am worried. The team are very fond of the DI. They'll want to know what's happened to him."

Birch looked away. "Let's get the facts first."

"Is Calladine working on some case that we're not aware of?" Ruth said.

"No. He is missing. Leave it at that for now."

The DCI went back to examining a file on her desk. She obviously wasn't going to say anything further. Ruth was dismissed.

None the wiser, Ruth went back to the incident room. They still had a murder to investigate, not that Ruth felt like getting stuck into it now. All she wanted to do was find Tom Calladine.

She looked around at the others. "Did the boss say he was going anywhere when he left?"

"No. Straight home was the order from Birch. He'd been going over the Costello file in readiness for the trial," Joyce said. "He was in his office most of the afternoon. It was only when he surfaced that I noticed the rash on his face. Once Birch saw him, she sent him home."

With so much happening, Ruth had forgotten about the trial. Vincent Costello had chanced his luck once too often, and this time there was enough evidence to put him away. Calladine was due to appear for the prosecution early next week.

Ruth stood still. Was that it? Had Costello arranged Tom's disappearance? Is that why Birch had been so cagey? Without a word to the others, Ruth went back to the DCI's office.

"The Costello trial, ma'am. Is it possible that Calladine's disappearance is connected?"

Birch said nothing.

"Costello still has his dodgy contacts. He could arrange for Calladine not to turn up in court. If that happened, is there any chance Costello could walk?"

Birch sighed. "You're not going to let this drop, are you?"

"I can't. If it was one of us, Tom wouldn't rest until he'd sorted it."

"Ruth, I am going to have to trust you. What I am about to tell you must go no further. Do you understand?"

Ruth nodded.

"You are right about the Costello angle. But it's not what you think. Calladine has not been kidnapped. We believe he's disappeared of his own volition."

"You think he's done a runner? That he doesn't want to give evidence?" How could Birch get it so wrong? It was obvious to Ruth what had happened. "But the blood, ma'am. I found his phone where he dropped it during a scuffle."

"You have no evidence of that."

"Forensics will get the evidence," Ruth insisted.

"Possibly. But it is our belief that the evidence will have been staged to confuse the issue."

Ruth couldn't believe what she was hearing. "There's blood, a lost phone and he's nowhere to be found! Tom wouldn't disappear and say nothing! It's plain what has happened. He's been taken. Nothing else makes any sense. He has a home, family and friends. Not to mention the job!"

"We don't like this any more than you, Ruth, but the fact remains. Calladine has chosen to disappear."

Ruth was mystified. "Why would the powers that be even think that of Tom?"

"There is a piece of this puzzle that you are unaware of . . ." Birch's voice faltered.

Moments ago, she'd been angry. Ruth had been afraid that she'd overstepped the mark. Now all that was gone. Birch looked decidedly nervous. "Go on, ma'am," Ruth said.

"Calladine has gone. If certain lines of enquiry go as we think they will, it is unlikely that he'll be back."

Ruth was aghast. Not be back? "You can't know that. What lines of enquiry?"

"I can't discuss it. Believe me, I'm not happy about this either."

"Why are you so sure that it's Tom who's in the wrong?"

"Because we've been given information. It comes from a reliable source and can be verified."

"What information?" Ruth asked.

"I can't discuss the details. But we believe he has disappeared so that he won't have to give evidence at the trial."

Ruth shook her head. "Tom would never do that!"

"I'm afraid he has," said Birch. "We suspect that he's thrown his lot in with that villain."

"It's a scam. Someone's trying to blacken his name."

"In that case, they are doing a good job of it. We have information that a sum of one hundred thousand pounds has been deposited in his bank account. I don't need to say that that information must not leave this room."

This took a second or two to sink in. A hundred thousand pounds, Ruth repeated to herself. The words made no sense. "Do you have proof of that?"

"Not yet. A warrant is being arranged to gain access to his account. Then we'll know for sure."

"You think Calladine took a bribe?" Shaking her head, Ruth stepped back from the desk. "You've taken some gossip as gospel. Why would you do that?"

"We have no choice. But it is *not* gossip. The source is trustworthy. For the time being, we are keeping an open mind. But the fact remains that Calladine cannot be found, or reached by phone. He has disappeared. That much is irrefutable."

"You don't know him at all, do you?" Ruth said almost in a whisper.

Birch was grim. "I know the facts, Sergeant."

"He's been set up. Tom would never take money to stay silent, I'd stake my life on it. You haven't even investigated properly yet. Do you think that because of his connection to Ray Fallon he is open to bribery and corruption at the hands of any passing villain!"

Ray Fallon had been one of Manchester's most notorious gangsters. And Calladine's cousin. Something the DI had found difficult to live down.

Now Birch was angry. Her expression was thunderous. "You would do well to remember your place," she said with feeling. "I am not the one in the wrong here."

"Neither is Tom Calladine. He's been kidnapped. It's as clear as daylight. This is Costello making sure he doesn't make it to the trial. He has engineered this. Tom is innocent. He is one of our own, for goodness sake!"

But Birch looked at her stonily. Whatever the DCI and her seniors had been told, it had to be pretty damning. Ruth wondered who their source was.

Birch tapped the file with a pen. "There will be a full investigation. An SIO has been appointed and will be arriving soon. Make him welcome, and make sure he gets all the help he needs. But the team must not know why he's here."

Ruth was reeling. This was some sort of nightmare. "How do I do that? The team will ask what he's doing here."

"Tell them he's looking at your current case."

"Who is it, ma'am?"

"DCI Greco."

Chapter 9

Birch had instructed Ruth not to tell the team. Even if she wanted to, she couldn't. Ruth didn't have the words. But what was she supposed to tell them about the imminent arrival of Greco?

Her head was all over the place. But one thing she was sure of, Calladine had not taken a bribe. That begged the question of what that much money was doing in his account? The only explanation she could come up with was Costello. What Ruth didn't understand was why Birch and those upstairs didn't see things the way she did.

She went slowly back to the incident room. "How are we doing?"

"No luck with tattoo parlours," Rocco said. "But I've had a closer look at the image Natasha gave us. I think it was done by an amateur."

"You're talking a friend? Someone with a DIY kit?"

"It would be a simple enough job," he said. "It's not a complicated design."

"It doesn't help us much." Ruth sat at her desk, feeling sick. She couldn't concentrate. Rocco was discussing his theories with Alice. They were keen, cracking on with the task in hand. All Ruth wanted to do was find Calladine.

"Joyce!" she called out. "Did the guv say anything about the Costello case? Give his opinion on the outcome, for example?"

Joyce shook her head. "He wasn't well. He didn't say a word for most of the afternoon. Just read through the file and then got off home after Birch told him to."

It didn't make any sense. She could understand Calladine being kidnapped and held until the court case was over. But why the money? Could Costello even lay his hands on that amount of cash these days? Most of the villain's wealth was derived from drug dealing. His bank accounts would have been frozen. But if not Costello, then who?

"What about the kid?" Rocco asked. "Do you think she's up to talking to us?"

"We can try. Will you ring her mum and arrange it?" Ruth checked her watch. Chloe Addison would still be in school. "Can I have a look at the George Norbury file? It's about all we've got to work with at the moment."

Ruth flicked through the pages but the words didn't make any sense. Norbury had confessed. That much was fact. But when he'd been arrested, he hadn't told them much, simply kept insisting that he'd murdered the woman. He didn't say how he carried out the killing or why he'd nailed the body to a lump of wood. What swung it in the end was evidence gathered from his flat. CSI found the branding iron, a knife, a box of nails and a claw hammer. Presented with these objects, they couldn't shut Norbury up. He told them everything. Coupled with the evidence, his confession was credible.

"We can go round any time after four," said Rocco. "The kid's been talking to her mother about her experience. Finding the dead woman upset her more than being taken by Johns."

"That's because the kids on that estate know Henry Johns. He's a big kid himself. They don't see him as a real threat."

Rocco nodded at the file on Ruth's desk. "Do you think the old case has any bearing on what we're dealing with?"

"I wish I knew. Julian is running more tests. We'll have to wait and see."

"Is he still locked up?" Rocco said. "I mean, he hasn't been let out early for good behaviour or something?"

"Unlikely, but we'll check." Ruth glanced at her watch. "Do you want to come and talk to Chloe with me, Alice?"

"She lives on the Hobfield?" Alice didn't look very enthusiastic.

"Yes. Heron House."

* * *

Alice shuddered. "This place gives me the creeps. It looks so bare. There isn't a tree or a patch of green in sight."

"The Hobfield has its problems, but there are some good people here too. The Addisons are a case in point," Ruth said.

"I wouldn't want to live here with a child. If the family had a house somewhere better, little Chloe wouldn't have got herself kidnapped."

As soon as Alice mentioned the word 'kidnapped,' Ruth's thoughts flew back to Calladine and his predicament. She had to do something. There was no way she could just let things lie. Ruth decided to pass by his street on her way home, and ask the neighbours if they'd seen anything.

The two detectives walked towards the entrance to the tower block.

"Chloe and her parents live on the second floor," Ruth said. "We go easy. It might be that we come back and talk to her another time. It's important that Chloe knows she can trust us."

"She may know nothing at all, Sarge," Alice said.

Chloe Addison was six years old. She was tall for her age and her dark hair was in pigtails. The detectives followed Mrs Addison and Chloe into the sitting room, the little girl clutching at her mother's skirt. Once they were seated, she peeped shyly at the two strange women.

"Do you remember being in the church, Chloe?" Alice asked.

The child nodded. "I didn't like it. Henry said I had to stay with him and he shouted at everyone. He didn't want to play that day."

"Does Henry usually play with the children?" Ruth asked.

"He organises games for the kids down in the square. He is a very gentle person as a rule. What happened the other day was totally out of character," Mrs Addison said.

"What else did you see?" Ruth asked.

"The lady."

"That can't have been very nice." Ruth knew she had to tread carefully here. The child probably didn't understand what she'd seen.

"She was dead. She should have been in a grave but she wasn't," Chloe stated.

A child's logic.

"Did you touch anything?" Ruth asked.

Chloe shook her head. "Everything was yucky."

"Did you see the pink teddy on the floor?" Ruth asked.

"At first it was on her arm. I knocked it off with a stick and it fell on the floor. It looked new so I picked it up. But I threw it away when I saw the blood."

As Alice had pointed out, George Norbury had placed the teddy on the victim's body. Chloe's information meant that the latest killing followed the same pattern.

Chapter 10

Calladine showered and dressed and then went downstairs. He still didn't feel right, but most of all he wanted to get out of here. There had to be a village nearby or another house or farm where he could get help. He had left work ill, so it was quite possible that his colleagues weren't even aware that he was missing. But Layla would realise. Surely, she would raise the alarm.

The downstairs rooms were furnished in the same style as the bedroom. Dark wood furniture, sofas that looked as if they'd come straight out of the fifties. The place had obviously been untouched for years. Bookshelves covered one entire wall. He searched them for anything that would help him get back or work out where he was. But there was nothing useful.

The woman who'd given him breakfast appeared in the doorway. Calladine turned towards her. "Where is this place?"

She gave him an enigmatic smile. "A long way away from where you want to be, Inspector Calladine."

"How far? Will you at least tell me that?" He watched her consider this.

"I've been told that it doesn't make much difference now. The damage has been done. You are some thirty miles north of Ullapool."

"Northern Scotland! How do you expect me to get home from here?" Calladine was horrified.

"I don't, because you aren't going anywhere."

"That's where you're wrong, lady. I'm leaving here today."

From one of the tables she picked up a small hand-bell. "I ring this and you'll be back in that bed the worse for wear. Now, you don't want that, do you?"

Calladine decided to ignore this for the time being. "There's someone else here?"

"Yes, and they won't take kindly to you giving me or them a hard time. Do as I say. Go to your room and stay there until I get word to release you."

"When will that be?"

She shrugged. "A day, a week. In truth, I have no idea."

"Who do you work for?"

"You don't really expect me to tell you that, do you?" she said.

"Can I have my stuff back? I have no money, no phone—"

"No! You're not going anywhere, so you don't need anything."

"I want to tell my family and friends at home that I'm okay." He didn't really believe she'd agree.

"They'll have to wait."

"Who put you up to this?" Calladine asked. "Surely you don't expect me to simply roll over and do nothing? Believe me, the moment the opportunity presents itself, I'll be gone. I'll walk out of here and make my own way back."

"That would be a foolish thing to do. The environment around here is harsh and unforgiving. This is the only dwelling for miles. There are no other houses or places to shelter. Set off on your own, get lost and you could easily freeze to death."

She was probably right. He knew very little about this immediate area. He did know that the Scottish Highlands were desolate in places. No wonder he wasn't being kept locked in the bedroom. There was little danger of him escaping and making it to safety. He studied the woman for a few moments, wanting to remember what she looked like. She didn't have a Scottish accent.

"You said that the damage has been done. What do you mean?" The more Calladine thought about it, the more he believed it had to be the work of Costello. The court case was looming, and although Calladine didn't consider his testimony to be of vital importance, perhaps Costello did.

"Not for me to say. But if you do get back, you'll find out soon enough."

The word 'if' bothered him. Did it mean they had no intention of letting him go? "Vinny Costello is at the bottom of this."

She smiled again. "I don't know who you're talking about."

Of course she did. But Calladine wasn't up to working it out. His head still hurt. He wanted to lie down again, rest up until he felt better. But his anger drove him forward. He had to at least try to escape.

"I need my things. I'll rip this place apart if I have to."

He meant it too. But she simply shrugged it off. "You don't have the strength. Apart from which, you'd be wasting your time. What you want isn't here. And I have no phone or money of my own to give you."

"How far to the nearest road?"

"Not far. At the end of that track." She nodded in the direction of the front gates.

"Is it a busy road?" he asked.

"It's hardly a road at all, one car's width that's all. We are hardly a large population up here so not many cars."

"Am I allowed outside? I wouldn't mind some fresh air." He wanted to have a look around, get his bearings.

"I don't see why not. As I just told you, you can't escape. The grounds are secure. There are high metal railings all around the garden and the gates are padlocked. But try anything clever and you'll spend the rest of your stay locked up."

"What about my coat? I was wearing an overcoat when I was attacked."

"I'm afraid it was covered in blood. The people who took you were a little overenthusiastic."

"Whatever they hit me with cut the back of my head open." He felt the area again. He'd been lucky. It could have been much worse.

She picked up a padded anorak that was lying on a chair and threw it at him. "Take this. It'll be more use. It's cold up here."

Calladine caught it, grunted and left the room. He was under no illusion, getting out of here would not be easy. Even if he did escape, he was still stranded. He had no money or phone, and had no idea what lay beyond those locked gates. Whoever had taken him wanted him well and truly out of commission.

Donning the anorak, he made his way through the house, into the kitchen and out of the back door. The gardens were huge, a vast swathe of green lawn surrounded by a border of spring bulbs. Trees around the perimeter hid a high metal fence. A gravel path led down one side of the lawn to a pair of hefty wrought iron gates. They were held together by a metal chain and padlocked. The woman hadn't been joking. Frustrated, Calladine grabbed one of the posts and gave the gate a shake. There was no way through on foot without a key for the padlock. But the chain might give if it was rammed with a vehicle. Who was he kidding, where would he get his hands on something hefty enough to do the job?

"What are you doing?"

The voice was deep and gruff. Calladine spun round. A heavily-built man stood looking at him, flexing his fists. Not the type you took on in Calladine's condition.

"Get back inside. There's nothing out here for you."

Calladine smiled at him. "Just getting familiar with the surroundings."

"Inside now, and cut the backchat. Try anything, attempt to get out of here, and you won't walk for a week."

"Mind if I stroll around the lawn?"

"Don't wind me up. Stay where I can see you."

The man strode away, making for a large garage. Calladine followed at a distance. There could be a vehicle in there. If he could find the keys, perhaps he could use it to get through those gates.

* * *

Ruth and Alice were back at the nick.

"Get anything useful?" Rocco asked.

"Chloe moved the teddy off the body onto the floor. The killer had left it wedged between her arm and her body," Ruth said.

"Same as Norbury then. Professor Batho wants to speak to you."

Ruth picked up the office phone and dialled Julian's number. She told him about the toy. "Might be worth dusting for prints."

"We will. But there is something even more interesting about it. It has a label. It's made by a small local company that makes soft toys and other baby stuff. Their workshop is in Hopecross. I took the liberty of ringing them. They only supply the toy shop in Lowermill, the one called 'Playstop.'"

"Thank you, Julian. I'll speak to them."

"Anything from Tom yet?"

Ruth had told him that Tom was asleep at Layla's and she hadn't wanted to disturb him. She could only keep that

56

up for so long. "I'll try him again later," she promised. Julian seemed happy with that, and at least it bought her a bit more time.

Ruth sat down at her desk. Come morning, DCI Stephen Greco would arrive. What then? She couldn't lie to the team. They'd see right through her. Apart from which, she needed their help. If they were to find Calladine, she'd have to tell Julian too. Perhaps if they worked together, under the radar, they might discover what was really going on. She was absolutely certain that Calladine hadn't taken a bribe. So who had put that money in his account?

Chapter 11

Calladine went back to his room. After a couple of hours' shuteye, he felt better, stronger. He got up and went to the window. The sun was setting. Reds and golds blended in the darkening sky, a colourful end to a bright, sunny day. At any other time, Calladine would have appreciated the view. Today, the only thing on his mind was escape.

He pulled on his shoes and grabbed the anorak. If he encountered the woman he'd tell her he was having a final stroll before dinner. He was in luck. She was nowhere to be seen. It crossed his mind that perhaps she didn't live in the house. Maybe she just came here to work — to cook and clean for the unfortunates that were brought here.

He crept towards the back door. It was unlocked. Across the garden, he could see a light on in the garage. The lump with the fists must still be working. Calladine edged slowly around the garage wall and peered in through the window. What he saw gladdened his heart. The truck was large, heavy. If he drove fast at those front gates he might just break through. But what to do about the lump? He was twice his size and built like a barn door. Calladine needed to catch him off guard. He searched around for something to hit him with.

Next to the garage was a small shed, unlocked and full of gardening equipment. Calladine picked up a spade. One clout delivered with force should do the job. All he had to do now was get the bugger to come outside.

He went back to the garage doors and stood to one side of them, in the shadows. Calladine was nervous and he still felt weak. If this didn't work, they might cut their losses and kill him. He closed his eyes. Whatever happened, he had to try. A piercing whistle plus a piece of rockery stone thrown at the door did the trick. The man rushed out.

Calladine's heart pounded. He watched the huge man stand and peer out into the darkness. After a few seconds, he grunted, turned and made to go back inside. Now. Calladine lashed out with the spade, and struck him just below the shoulder blades. The lump roared, balled his fists and turned on him. Calladine was horrified. If that blow hadn't stopped him, what would?

He backed off slowly.

The lump struck out with his right fist, catching Calladine in the eye. He reeled back, still clinging onto the spade. Ignoring the pain and using every bit of strength he had left, he lashed out again. The spade hit the big man on his upper arm, making him howl. Calladine quickly followed this with a blow to the side of the head and the man slumped to the ground.

Calladine bent over him. The lump was out cold. This was the only chance he was going to get. He went into the garage. Luck was on his side. The keys were still in the ignition, the truck facing the garage doors. Hauling himself into the driving seat he started the engine. Slowly he inched outside and drove towards the gate. Still a distance away, he put his foot down and the truck hurtled forward. He hit the gate hard, and was thrown against the windscreen. Calladine hardly felt the impact, but the truck had stalled. The gate was still locked tight. He took a quick look in the rear mirror. No sign of the lump. He started the engine, reversed back several metres and sped towards the gate a second time. There was a scream, as metal tore at metal. The chain gave way, and the gate swung open. He was out!

He drove, hardly daring to look in the rear mirror in case someone was following him. But the road was empty. Calladine had no awareness of passing time and no idea how far he'd gone. He leaned forward and squinted over the steering wheel. The road was narrow and there was no lighting. He hadn't seen a house or farm anywhere near, and he had no idea if he was even going in the right direction. But whatever happened, it was preferable to another night in that house.

Suddenly the engine made a clanging noise. It began to rattle, and steam rose from under the bonnet. Another few metres and finally the engine stalled. It was goosed, going no further. That must have been what the lump was doing, fixing the thing.

He had no alternative but to dump the truck and continue on foot. Not a great prospect. It would be warmer to stay in the vehicle, but that thug was bound to come looking and Calladine couldn't take that risk. He would know these roads. Finding the abandoned truck would not be difficult.

The night was pitch black. Calladine couldn't see a light anywhere. His head pounded. He was too old for this fighting lark. Plus, he'd had nothing to eat since the toast the woman had given him that morning. But the most pressing danger was the cold.

Calladine started down the lane. There was no footpath. Every so often the clouds in the night sky parted and moon illuminated the way ahead. The lane abutted steep hills on one side and a drop on the other. Slip up and he might never be found. He was so wrapped up in his worries that he didn't hear the Land Rover come up behind him. The voice made him jump. Had the big man recovered and come after him? And then his heart leapt. He was about to be rescued.

"You okay, mister? Not a good idea to wander around out here after dark, you know. Where are you headed?"

Calladine beamed up at the driver. "Am I glad to see you! The truck I was driving broke down, and I was facing the prospect of a night outside."

The man smiled. "Well, you look mighty relieved, I must say. Got yourself lost, did you?"

"I'm making for Ullapool," Calladine said.

The man laughed. "That's one helluva walk. Why didn't you stay with your truck? Someone would have found you in the morning."

"I had no choice, believe me. But it's a long story."

"Get in. I'm going to Ullapool to pick up my daughter from the station. You can tell me your story on the way."

His rescuer introduced himself as Jim Munro. Unable to believe his luck, Calladine opened the vehicle door. As he hauled himself into the passenger seat, the first thing Calladine asked was if Jim had a mobile he could use. "I must contact the local police urgently, get them to raid that house, arrest the people there."

"I have, but there is no signal out here. I'm afraid you've no choice but to wait until you get to Ullapool."

"How long will it take?" Calladine didn't want the pair he'd met absconding.

"Another ten minutes and we'll be there. Tell me what happened to you."

Calladine gave the man a brief rundown, including a description of the huge old house.

"From what you say, it sounds like you were kept at Moortop Manse. Weird place. Folk around here have no idea who actually owns the old house. It used to be the home of the McCloud family. After the old woman died it was sold off."

"Once I get back, I'll find out all I can about that place." Calladine was determined that whoever had kidnapped him wasn't going to get away with it.

"I'll drop you off at the 'Highland Laddie.' You can use the phone and rest up. It's a good little pub and they have rooms to let. Morag does a mean supper. Bet you've not eaten all day, have you?"

"Thanks, Jim. If you hadn't come along, God knows what I'd have done."

* * *

Jake said he wanted to talk about the move, but Ruth wasn't keen. She'd arrived home late, with too much on her mind. Harry, their toddler son, was teething and consequently cranky.

"All I want is to settle Harry, shower and then get to bed. If we start debating your career, we'll be at it till morning," Ruth said.

Ruth had plans for the following day. Before the team went into the nick, she wanted them to meet up at a local café and discuss what had happened to Calladine. That way, they wouldn't be too surprised when Greco turned up.

"The school rang me today. They need to know my decision by the end of the week," Jake said.

Ruth was only too aware that time was running out. She didn't need to have it thrust down her throat every time they spoke.

"The move will be good for all of us, Ruth. I really want this."

The problem was, Ruth didn't. But if she refused, she was certain it would mean the end of their relationship. The prospect was horrendous. For her sake and Harry's, she couldn't contemplate a life without Jake. "I'll sleep on it," she said. "Tomorrow we'll talk, I promise."

"We could be there for the start of the new academic year in September. That gives us six months to find a new home."

Jake was jumping the gun — again. Had he even been listening? "You're presuming I'll agree to go. This is massive for me, Jake. I've spent my entire life in this area. I have my career here, friends."

Jake opened his mouth, but the ring of Ruth's mobile cut him off. She went out onto the landing to take the call.

"Listen closely lady and don't interrupt." The voice was male, rough and not one she recognised. "You and that copper friend of yours will keep your mouths shut. Come looking, turn up the heat and you'll both regret it."

There was a pause. Ruth didn't understand what this was about. "Who is this?"

There was a harsh laugh. "Like I'd tell you. Be warned, if that DI of yours does anything about what happened to him there will be consequences."

"Making threats against police officers is a serious offence," she warned him. "This call will be traced." Her voice was sharp, Ruth was angry.

"No, it won't, this mobile is single use." He laughed. "Can't be too careful. And in case you're in any doubt about how serious this is, that's a nice nursery your boy goes to. Shame security is so lax in the playground. I've had a look for myself. Snatching a kid would be easy. That copper friend of yours has family too. Do both of yourselves a favour, leave it alone, say nothing."

At that he hung up. Ruth felt sick, dazed. She had no idea what the man was going on about, but from the tone of his voice, he'd meant every word. What should she do? She was still deliberating this when her mobile rang again.

"Tom!" she shouted. "Where the hell are you? I've been going crazy with worry."

"It's quite a tale," he said. "But I'm fine now. I'm in Ullapool at a pub. I'm just about to raise the troops, get the bastards who kidnapped me arrested."

Now she understood what the previous call was all about. "Don't," she said. "I've just had a call from a man I don't know. He threatened to snatch Harry if we do anything about what happened to you."

"Did he give any clue who he was?"

"No. But he was one scary man. He meant it, Tom. Leave telling the police for now. It's too risky, just come home and then we'll decide what to do."

The phone went silent. Ruth knew that Tom was considering what she'd told him.

"We can't do that, Ruth. It's too dangerous." He said soberly. "The people who took me are determined and ruthless. You have no guarantees. Tomorrow you tell Birch about the phone call. You tell her where I was held, the place is called Moortop Manse, it's north of Ullapool. She can arrange to have the place raided. You tell her about threat made against Harry too. She will arrange proper protection. It is the only way."

"What do I tell her about you?"

"I should be back sometime tomorrow. I'll speak to her myself, explain what happened."

"It's not that simple, Tom. You're in real bother."

"Why?" he said. "It's not my fault I was kidnapped."

"There is another aspect to this this. You disappear, leave no word . . ." She paused.

"Go on. I sense a punchline coming."

"Birch is saying that someone put small fortune into your bank account. Birch and the rest of them think you took a bribe. You have online banking, don't you? You need to check it out as soon as you can."

"You're joking!" Calladine said.

"Not about this, I'm not. They're investigating you as we speak."

So that's what this had been all about. Blackening his name. But why?

"I'll check it on the phone when I get one. I'll text you."

"What do I tell Birch about you? She will ask where you are, where you phoned me from."

"Tell her I was vague, that we got cut off, and you don't know where I was heading for. The important things are arresting the people at that house and keeping Harry safe. I'll come back and take care of myself."

"They made threats against your family too. What about Zoe?"

"Tell Birch. For now don't say anything to Zoe. I'll speak to her."

"I'll meet you at the station," Ruth said. "I'll find you somewhere quiet and out of the way to stay. Perhaps Doc Hoyle would put you up? Once you're safely back, we'll talk."

"For now, I need you to bail me out. The people who took me, they've kept my things I've lost my phone and my wallet. That's why I rang you first before contacting the police. I want you to speak to the landlord, pay for my room and get him to give me some cash, enough to get back."

"Okay, put him on."

The landlord agreed to help. He took enough money from Ruth via debit card to pay for the room and give Calladine the cash he needed for the train fare home and to buy a cheap pay-as-you-go mobile from the small supermarket in the town.

"I'll text you when I get into Manchester Piccadilly."

Chapter 12

Day 3

In a narrow back street behind Leesdon bus station, there was a small café. It was an old-fashioned greasy spoon, with old Formica topped tables and steamed-up windows, but it served the best fried breakfast for miles around.

Ruth had texted the team and asked them to meet her there at seven thirty. She'd also invited Doc Hoyle to join them. Sebastian Hoyle had been the senior pathologist attached to Leesworth hospital. Before privatisation and the advent of the Duggan, Doc Hoyle had dealt with all the post-mortems. Over the years, he and Tom Calladine had become fast friends, and Ruth was hoping he'd help them now.

Rocco was the first to arrive, muffled up against the unseasonal frost they'd had overnight. "My mum's complaining that it's killed off all the buds on her hydrangeas. Simple problems. Wish I lived in her world."

Ruth grinned at him. "No, you don't. You'd be bored. You'd miss the drama of the job. You thrive on it."

Alice and Joyce arrived together, followed by Doc Hoyle.

"What's this all about?" he asked. "Don't tell me — it's our missing friend, isn't it? Julian told me you couldn't find him. What's happened?"

Ruth merely handed a slip of paper to Alice. "Write down what you want to eat and pass it on."

"You're not having much," Rocco said when his turn came. "Just tea and toast. No appetite, eh? Clandestine early morning meeting. Must be summat up. You've got me on edge now."

Ruth waited for the tea to arrive before she spoke. "Tom isn't at home recuperating. He never got the chance. He was attacked outside his house and kidnapped." Everyone gasped. "He's okay now. He escaped and is on his way back from the north of Scotland. I'll be picking him up later."

"Why take him up there?" Rocco asked. "It makes no sense. And who took him?"

"Someone wanted him out of the way. We have no idea who or why." Ruth could see they were having trouble taking all of this in. "While Tom was being held, a great deal of money found its way into his bank account. Birch still doesn't have proof of that — the warrant is taking its time to come through. But last night, Tom checked online and confirmed to me that it's true. He is one hundred grand richer than he was before the kidnapping. Birch is convinced he's taken a bribe. I'm guessing she suspects that he's in cahoots with Costello. Remember, the trial's coming up—"

"No! No way." Rocco was shaking his head. "The boss would never do that! Birch is barking up the wrong tree. Why would she even consider it? What evidence does she have?"

"Calladine would never do anything of the sort," Joyce said. "He's as honest as the day is long. Birch needs to think again!"

"I agree, but I can't do much on my own. I've tried to speak to Birch, but I'm a voice in the wilderness. That's why we're here. I want us to work together to find out what really happened. I'm also thinking it was Vinny Costello, but not the way Birch sees it. I'm sure Costello set this up to make Tom look bad, and to stop him giving evidence."

"Would Costello be able to get his hands on that much money?" Rocco asked. "You know the law and the proceeds of crime. I doubt Costello has done an honest day's work in his life. Won't his ill-gotten fortune be well out of his reach?"

"He may have offshore accounts that no one knows about." Privately, Ruth doubted this, but they had to follow the money trail. Until they did that, it was all speculation.

"Tom won't be allowed back to work while he's under suspicion," Doc Hoyle said. "They'll appoint someone to investigate. You've presumed it's down to Costello, but you can't be sure. I don't want to tell you how to do your jobs, but that needs establishing first."

Ruth sighed wearily. "I know that. But who else can it be? He and Tom have plenty of history between the pair of them. Tom is giving evidence against him this coming week. And they *have* appointed someone to investigate. DCI Stephen Greco arrives this morning. That's partly why I wanted to see you all. I'm not supposed to tell you why he's with us, but that would never have worked. It was Birch's idea, not mine."

"Greco, of all people!" Rocco said. "The boss isn't too fond of him and vice versa. As I recall, last time they met they almost came to blows."

Ruth looked at Alice. "Greco will have Tom's office. He'll need someone to help him. You'd be good at that. Greco will appreciate your methodical approach and organisation."

"My nerdy ways, you mean." Alice wasn't smiling.

"He's a stickler for doing things properly," Ruth said. "He does his research. You'll work well together. You'll also be able to keep us informed of what he turns up."

Alice's face darkened even further. "I don't know if I can do that. I mean, if I'm working with the man, and he trusts me to keep everything confidential."

"I understand, Alice. But you have to ask yourself where your loyalties lie. I'm sure I speak for the others when I say that we are one hundred percent behind Tom Calladine. We'll do everything we can to prove his innocence, and find who set him up. I realise you're new to the team, but you have to trust us."

"You want me to work with Greco, and report back to you about his findings?"

Ruth nodded. "Exactly."

"Can I think about it?"

"Don't take too long." Ruth checked her watch. There was very little time. She'd just have to trust that Alice saw sense. The others were listening to them while they ate.

Rocco nudged Alice. "He's not the 'Mr Perfect' you think he is, you know."

"I've heard people speaking about him. He's highly regarded. He must be good." Alice frowned at him.

"He got his DC, Grace Harper, up the duff." Rocco said. "Have you heard that one? A few days in Brighton, one drunken night, that's all it took."

Alice looked at the others. "Is that right?"

"But we don't know the whole story, so it's best not to spread gossip." Ruth glowered at Rocco. "Grace Harper and Greco were an item, I believe. I'm not sure that they didn't get engaged at one point."

"Not pregnant now though, is she?" Rocco persisted. "No more engagement either. Tells you a lot, that does, both about the situation and the man. You have to stick with us, Alice. We need Calladine back where he belongs.

Quite apart from him being a friend, the alternatives don't bear thinking about."

"Rocco's right," Ruth said. "And, please, no one else must know that Tom's escaped. The people who took him'll be looking. His life could be in danger."

"Tom didn't take any bribe," the doc said firmly. "If it was money he wanted, he could have had a fortune by throwing in his luck with that cousin of his years ago. Apart from which, that newfound family of his is worth a fortune. What are you going to do with him once he's back?"

"I was hoping he could stay with you. He can't go home, the kidnappers will be watching." Ruth crossed her fingers under the table.

Doc Hoyle nodded. "Okay, bring him to mine. I live at the back end of nowhere. He'll be well out of the way there."

* * *

Back at the station, Ruth went straight to Birch's office. "I've had a call from DI Calladine, ma'am."

"Where is he?"

"He was kidnapped and taken to a house in the north of Scotland." She handed Birch a slip of paper with the name and partial address on it. "It's north of Ullapool, that's all I know. But local police will no doubt be familiar with it."

"You want me to mobilise the force in a different area on the say-so of a DI currently under investigation?"

"Yes, ma'am. Last night I also received an anonymous call from a man who threatened harm to my son and DI Calladine's daughter if I did anything about what I knew."

"If that's true, then it changes things. I'll do as you suggest. I take it Calladine has escaped. Whoever was holding him must have realised that he'd contact you. Where is he now?"

"I've no idea," Ruth lied. "The reception was bad. I could hardly hear him, eventually we were cut off altogether."

Ruth watched Birch consider this. "I'll organise an immediate watch on your son and Zoe Calladine. Does Zoe know?"

"I don't think so, ma'am. The DI won't want to frighten her."

"Nonetheless she needs to be told. I also need a breakdown of where your son is and who he is with during the times you're working."

"I'll do you an itinerary."

"Make it quick. This needs sorting quickly."

* * *

Stephen Greco was sure the Leesdon team didn't want him in their old-fashioned, poky building any more than he wanted to be here. The heating wasn't up to scratch, and it was cold. The windows were double glazed but the installation was out of the ark. The unit in Calladine's office had a gale blowing through it.

"DS Bayliss will make sure you get all the help you need, Stephen. Any hesitation, just let me know," Rhona Birch said.

That, Greco presumed, was the DCI's idea of a welcome. He sighed. He knew the score. The top brass had looked at this case and condemned Calladine without benefit of trial. Well, he wouldn't make the same mistake.

It was eight thirty before the team began to arrive. Rocco was first. He was studying the incident board when Greco called out to him.

"Late start. Is this the usual routine?"

"No, sir. We had a case meeting over breakfast. We've got a perplexing murder on our hands. Not much to go on and as yet no ID for the victim."

Greco stared at the incident board. The case looked dreadful, but it was the board itself that irritated him. The images, pinned up haphazardly, had messily-written notes beside them, all in different colours. Some were blue, some red. Not the way he worked.

"A while before she was found, by the look of the body," Greco said.

"Yes, and not much to go on. I'm about to go and interview the owner of a local business." Rocco meant the toy shop. "DS Bayliss won't be long. She's right behind me."

"Do you know why DI Calladine isn't at work?"

"He's ill, sir. Shingles, I believe."

The young detective looked away and shuffled his feet. Greco wasn't stupid. They knew. Ruth Bayliss must have told them. Greco turned on his heel and went back into Calladine's office. The Costello file was still on his desk where he'd left it, but the paperwork from inside it was missing.

"You've arrived." Ruth stood at the door, smiling. She came in and closed the door behind her. "I know why you're here. I had a word with DCI Birch about DI Calladine being missing. I'm also aware of what she thinks. I must make it clear from the start that I do *not* believe that Tom took a bribe."

Greco considered this. "I'm starting from a neutral position, neither believing nor disbelieving. The warrant isn't in yet anyway, so it's all still conjecture. I'll do my best to root out the truth, and I'm hoping you'll help me."

Ruth nodded. "As much as I can."

"You can start by not discussing this any further with your colleagues."

"I can't promise that. We work closely together on the most horrific crimes. We're fond of each other. Tom is well respected. The team want him back."

Greco frowned. He envied Calladine. He doubted that his own team felt the same about him, particularly not now, after what happened with Grace.

"Currently we have a challenging case on our hands," Ruth said. "We are short staffed, but I've asked DC Alice Bolshaw to work with you. She's very good and thorough."

"Thank you. Send her in and we'll get started."

Chapter 13

The Bentley glided to the front of Heron house and came to a stop. A group of lads who'd been idling at the entrance moved out of the way sharpish. The car belonged to Miles Erskine, but that wasn't widely known. All the Hobfield residents knew was that the posh limo belonged to the top man around there. Most didn't ask questions. Experience had taught them it was better not to know.

But Newt knew. He knew exactly who and what Miles Erskine was. To Newt, he was a sure-fire way of getting his hands on a lot of money. He stepped out of the shadow cast by the tower block and strolled towards the car.

"Get in. You all set?" a voice said from the back.

Newt sat in front, next to the driver. The voice from the back belonged to Miles himself. This made Newt nervous. The villain didn't like appearing in public and usually sent one of his thugs to do business. The operation must be big if he was here in person.

Newt nodded. "Ready to go, boss."

"There's been no money from you for days."

Newt's stomach was turning somersaults. "I had expenses. The new people, they wanted something up front. Given the size of the operation, like, I thought it only fair. Show goodwill and all that." A bluff, but Newt hoped Miles would accept the excuse. He didn't want to drop Alenka in it. She was quiet for now, but if she felt threatened, she'd tell the police. That'd make Miles angry, and do Newt no good. But he wasn't about to take a battering on her account either. He was in luck. Miles didn't appear particularly interested in the details.

"I hope you've chosen your people carefully. As you say, this is a big one. I stand to make a great deal of money and I want everything to run smoothly. I will *not* tolerate any cock-ups from the likes of you. D'you understand?"

Newt nodded.

"Delivery'll be at seven tonight. The merchandise is meth and spice. You'll get rid of the lot. You know your customers and what they want. You won't have long — I'll be back tomorrow for what's mine."

"No probs, Miles."

The man smiled coldly at Newt. "There'd better not be. I've got a new supplier, and I've made a huge investment. I can get my hands on all the dope my operatives can sell. My people have worked hard, sorted every little detail. My network has spread fast. It now reaches out all over Manchester and beyond. I've had to grease a lot of palms and that's cost me. Let me down, and you'll become another unfortunate statistic. Get me, Newt?"

"You can count on me, Miles. I know what I'm doing."

"Good, because things'll go badly for you if you mess up. Now get out."

The car drove off. Newt heaved a sigh of relief. He'd dodged one there, saved Alenka's skin — this time. She owed him. He'd make sure the bitch understood her position. She was going to work for him whether she liked it or not.

* * *

"The shop's on the High Street. Parking's a problem round here. Keep your eyes peeled," Ruth said, driving slowly.

Lowermill was a lot smaller than Leesdon. The main street was full of eateries — a tapas bar, numerous tea shops, a chippy and a huge Chinese restaurant. Behind all these were a library and the museum. The only parking space was up by the swimming pool, a fair walk away.

"There, alongside the market stalls." Rocco pointed.

She grunted. "Double yellows."

"Stick something on the windscreen. We're police, don't forget."

"Why's this place so busy?" Ruth said irritably.

"Market day."

"There are only three stalls! And one of them hasn't bothered. This place gets worse. How people who work here manage is a mystery to me."

Ruth was on edge. Greco hadn't said much. He was a fair man, but neither of them knew who they were up against. Someone had planted that money. What else had they done? Then there was the problem of Alice. Perhaps it hadn't been such a good idea to have her working with Greco. They were alike in many respects. God help them all if she and Greco hit it off. Alice wouldn't know which way to turn.

"The Playstop's over there." Rocco pointed to a colourful shop window. "I've got the photo." He tapped his overcoat pocket.

"Let's hope they remember something useful. We really could do with wrapping this up. And I have to admit, my mind isn't really on the job. Not with what's happening to Tom."

Rocco grinned. "Thought this was your opportunity to shine."

"I'm far too worried to shine at anything right now. I'm stumbling my way through this case. We've got Birch on our backs. She's expecting solid progress by the end of the day. If not, we'll get landed with Long. If Greco doesn't prove Tom's innocence, and Long takes over, I'll seriously consider that offer Jake has from the school down south."

Rocco looked at her. "You can't leave us, Ruth. If the boss doesn't come back, we'll need you more than ever."

"I'm flattered, really I am, but I have my own sanity to consider. We just have to find the evidence that'll clear his name."

The shop was a delight, full of toys of all kinds. Many of them were handmade and expensive. Flora Godfrey, the owner, was only too pleased to help. She recognised the pink teddy straight away.

She smiled. "A local woman made these. Currently she's doing a range of farm animals for us." She picked up a pink piglet and a fluffy lamb. "See? Sweet, aren't they?"

Ruth tapped the image of the teddy. "We want to know who bought these."

"Because most of our range is unusual, that particular item wasn't that popular. You can get pink teddies at any toyshop. Folk prefer these." She shook one of the lambs. "We don't stock the teddies any more. But a year ago, we had a dozen made. It was one of our first stock items." She reached under the counter and took out a sales ledger. "It was a sale-or-return arrangement as I recall. We sold only three, and the rest I gave back."

"Who bought those three?" Ruth asked.

"They went to the States. A woman took them for her granddaughters. Triplets, she said. They all had to have the same. See, I made a note in the book."

Not sold locally then. Ruth sighed.

"Can I have the name of the woman who made them?" asked Rocco. He looked at Ruth. "It's possible she sold the rest herself or gave them away."

Ruth should have thought of that, but her mind was elsewhere.

"Her name's Angie Carson. She lives on the Hobfield. Heron House."

They left the shop and walked back to the car.

"We'll go and find her," Ruth said. "It's highly likely she sold or gave them away round the estate."

Rocco sighed. "Here we go again. No matter what we find ourselves involved in, it always comes back to that damned estate."

Ruth managed to raise a smile. "We get a name off her and we're on our way."

Ruth heard someone call her name.

It was Jo Brandon, Tom's daughter's partner. She was an estate agent, and had an office in Leesdon. She was clutching a file of paperwork. She must be valuing a property, Ruth guessed. Bad luck, bumping into her. Ruth was hoping to avoid awkward questions from Tom's family.

"Is Tom alright? He rang Zoe last night, but the chat was garbled. He kept going on about how he was okay and on his way home. She said he wasn't making much sense."

"The shingles has laid him low. He still has a fever. I can't get much sense out of him either," she smiled. "A few more days and he'll bounce back," Ruth said.

"Zoe even rang the station and spoke to that DCI of yours, but she was no help at all."

Zoe obviously didn't know about the protection yet. "Tell Zoe not to worry. I might pop round and see him myself later. I'll get him to ring her, put her mind at rest."

Ruth saw the look. Jo didn't believe her.

"Tom told Zoe he'd been away due to a work thing. You're telling me he's ill. Is he in trouble?"

Ruth tried to look assured but failed. "It's something and nothing. There really is no need to worry. We're sorting it."

Chapter 14

Greco and Alice were closeted in Calladine's office, sitting on either side of the desk and ploughing through Costello's bank records. As far as they could tell, the villain had once had a fortune, but not anymore. Prior to being apprehended, he'd made a number of bad investments. He certainly had nothing like the hundred thousand that was languishing in DI Calladine's account.

Greco was finding it difficult to concentrate. The office was an alien environment, and nowhere near up to his standard of cleanliness. There were dirty teacups on the windowsill, and old sandwich cartons containing mouldy bread in the bin. Calladine had left a pile of papers on top of the filing cabinet. Greco had taken hot water and bleach to the desktop before starting to work. It was distracting. If he was forced to spend any longer here, then the office would have to be thoroughly cleaned. There were photographs too, people Greco didn't know.

"Who's the young woman?" he asked.

"Zoe. DI Calladine's daughter."

"And the others?"

Alice peered. "That old black-and-white one is his parents, I think."

"A family man, then?" Greco said.

"In some respects. I don't know the boss as well as the others, but his family life isn't as simple as it seems from these pictures. I've picked up that much in the time I've been here. His daughter wasn't in his life until just a few years ago. I said that the couple in the black-and-white photo were his parents, but actually the woman isn't his birth mother. When you get down to it, he's one huge complication."

"Families can be complicated." There was a note of resignation in his voice. He looked up. "We could always go and see Costello. Ask the man himself. Fancy a trip to Strangeways?"

Alice frowned. "If the money is down to him, he's hardly going to admit it."

"A face to face chat might get us somewhere. We need to ascertain if he has other accounts overseas. We know about a couple," he tapped the file Alice was preparing, "but there could be more."

She still looked dubious. "And you think he'll talk?"

"The case against Costello is serious. But there may be some leeway for us to do a deal if he's prepared to help. I'll speak to my contact at the CPS. They might also be able to confirm how important DI Calladine's testimony is to the case."

"Do you want me to arrange the visit to the prison?" Alice said.

Greco nodded. "Yes. We have to interview him in any event. Make it soon."

Greco wanted to get home. He had no intention of staying in Leesdon any longer than he had to. Alice was okay. In different circumstances, he would have enjoyed working with her. She paid attention and was meticulous. But he didn't like working in this office, or the station. Besides, he had put in for a transfer to another area. He had yet to discuss this with his super and needed to remedy that quickly. It was a pity, the task force he headed was getting results. But since the affair with Grace Harper and the loss of her baby, he couldn't remain. Greco felt he'd lost all credibility with his team.

While he was ruminating, Alice had made the call.

"Tomorrow morning, sir. That okay?"

"I'll speak to the CPS before we go." He looked at her. "You're new to the team here, aren't you? How are you getting on?"

Alice smiled. "I've actually met them before, on a previous case when I was a student."

"They're very close. They keep things tight, I've heard. DI Calladine works very differently from me. I've also heard that his team are fond of him."

"That's true," she said.

"Is that why they've asked you to work with me, because you're the new girl?"

Alice flushed slightly. His question had obviously embarrassed her. "Possibly. Both Ruth and Rocco would be too biased. They've been through a lot with Calladine and they trust him completely. I know they don't believe he's done anything wrong. They certainly don't believe he's taken a bribe. Ruth reckons he's been set up for some reason."

"She may be right. And if she is, we need to work out why. On the other hand, Calladine is coming up to retirement age. Perhaps someone made him an offer that was simply too tempting."

* * *

Ruth parked the car in front of Heron House. "We'll speak to Angie Carson, and then get back to the nick," she said. "Leaving Greco with the place to himself makes me nervous. He's working in Tom's office. He could find anything. We should have searched the place ourselves first. If someone can plant a small fortune in his bank, goodness knows what might they have put in his office."

She got out of the car and stood in the concrete square staring up at the block of flats. "It's rumoured that this little lot is coming down. Several new low-rise blocks and houses were supposed to be built on the site of the old cotton mill on the Oldston Road."

"Hasn't come to much. It'll be money," Rocco said. "Leesworth Council can barely afford to pay its staff wages these days."

Ruth shook her head. "Nothing to do with the council. Erskine Construction was earmarked for the project, but it's all been shelved for the time being. The old mill has gone into production again."

"Oh? What sort of production?"

"Cotton spinning. And it's being sent on to Burnley for weaving, just like the old days. Looks like Cottonopolis could make a comeback." Ruth smiled.

Rocco snorted. "You don't really believe that, do you? It'd take some heavy investment to get anything major started around here."

"I know, but it's providing a few much-needed jobs for the older generation."

Rocco laughed. "They'll be the only ones with any experience."

Ruth looked away. "My granny worked in a cotton mill. It's what killed her in the end. She was bad with her chest."

Angie Carson lived on the fifth floor of Heron House. She stood at the door and looked them up and down. "You're police." And then she smiled. "You get to know living in this place."

Ruth returned the smile. "We'd like to ask you about the soft toys you make."

"Why?" Angie asked. "Not against the law, is it?"

"No, not at all," Ruth said. "You made some pink teddy bears for Playstop. The owner told us that she only sold three and you took the rest back. Can you tell us what you did with them?"

Angie Carson stood aside. "You'd better come in." The flat was small and fairly dark, but neat enough. "Now you're asking me something. How do you expect me to remember that? I dish them out to my nieces and my friends' kids, for birthdays and such."

"Do you know if they still have them?"

She shrugged. "No idea. They're only little teddy bears."

"Can you compile a list of names for us?" Rocco asked.

"Now you're asking something! Nieces and nephews fine, but how am I supposed to remember every little kid I've handed one to?"

"Write down as many as you can recall," Rocco told her. "A uniformed officer will collect it later today. Could you have given some to people who weren't friends or family? Or maybe one or two of them got lost or stolen," Ruth said.

Angie laughed. "We're talking about small stuffed toys. Who'd want to steal one? They're not worth anything."

"We've found one at a crime scene. Hence our interest," Rocco said.

Angie shuddered. "A crime scene? How awful! How did one of my teddies get there? Now you've got me thinking."

"Anything you remember would be a great help," Rocco said.

"I did give a bagful to a charity shop in the town. They were asking specifically for toys. I'd hoped Playstop would keep the orders coming, so I'd stockpiled."

Ruth groaned inwardly. That meant anyone could have bought one.

She and Rocco left Heron House and made their way across the bare expanse of concrete back to the car.

"Is it worth asking at the charity shops?" Rocco asked.

Ruth shook her head. "We'll send a uniform, but I won't hold my breath."

On their way out of the estate, Ruth saw a group of kids surrounding a young mum pushing a pram. They were giving her a hard time, shouting and swearing at her. They ran around the pram, poking their fingers at the child.

"They need a lesson in manners." Ruth stopped the car and took off in their direction, in just the right mood to blast the lot of them. But the kids scarpered.

The young mum was crying.

"They didn't harm you or the child, did they?" Ruth said. The child, a little girl, was sitting up in the pram, screaming.

"No, they were just being cheeky." The mother attempted a smile.

Ruth frowned. "It looked a bit worse than that to me. Did they want something in particular? Were they trying to rob you?"

"No, nothing like that."

Rocco approached them. "Do you live in the block?" He was pointing at Heron House. "I'll give you a hand up with the pram if you want."

"We're police. We don't wish you any harm." Ruth had picked up on the girl's accent. She was obviously foreign, maybe Eastern European? "Where are you from?"

"Slovenia," she replied.

Ruth smiled at her. "You must find Leesdon very different."

The young woman nodded. "It always seems very busy, but I prefer it."

Rocco, who had gone off to call the lift, called out that it had arrived.

"If you have any more trouble from those kids, give us a ring at the station," Ruth said. "What's your name?"

"Why? Is it important?" The young woman looked fearful.

"No. Just being friendly. Here, take my card in case you ever need to talk." Ruth handed her a card.

"I am Ingrid. Ingrid Plesec." The young woman turned and pushed her pram towards the block.

Ruth watched her go, shaking her head. "We're far too busy for all this stuff. I'll get uniform to keep an eye out. Those kids that were bothering her looked like a rough lot." She checked her watch. "I'm picking Tom up from Piccadilly soon. But remember, Rocco. Not a word to anyone. He'll be keeping under the radar for a while yet. Doc Hoyle lives in Hopecross. The locals joke that it's the end of the world. No one ever goes there."

Chapter 15

"I'm going to have a word with that contact of mine from the CPS," Greco said. "Robert Galt. He's a lawyer. After that, I'll be going straight home. We'll leave for Strangeways at ten in the morning."

He was hoping that Robert Galt would be able to tell him something useful. And he needed a break. The atmosphere in Leesdon station was oppressive and it was doing him no good at all. He picked up his briefcase and left.

Greco's mind just wasn't on the assignment he'd been landed with. He was anxious about what was happening back at his own station, Oldston. His name was mud there. If the transfer came through, he wouldn't stay a moment longer than necessary. He'd worry about how to square it with the super when it happened. He'd had to have heard by now and was no doubt itching to have a word. Grace wouldn't be happy. But his main concern had to be the welfare of his daughter, Matilda. Since their breakup, she'd been missing Grace and playing with her daughter, Holly. What they both needed right now was a new start. A job in a less hectic station, with a lighter workload, would give him more time with Matilda.

Robert Galt had an office in the city centre, around the corner from the Crown Court. Greco had had dealings with him in the past and had found him to be fair minded and friendly. He was a tall man with dark hair, always impeccably dressed. He and Greco often met to discuss the cases they were involved in.

Galt shook his hand and invited him to come into his office. "You're interested in the Vincent Costello case? We've put in the hours on that one, believe me. We're leaving nothing to chance this time. The evidence has stacked up, and we've finally got him nailed. I can't see how any jury would fail to convict."

Galt's office was on the top floor of a high-rise block in central Manchester. It had wonderful views over the city and the blue-grey hills beyond.

The two men sat down. "So how can I help?" Galt asked.

"I want to know how important DI Tom Calladine's testimony is to the case. It could be relevant to another one we're working on." Greco deliberately kept it brief.

"The two have history, I know that much. A case that DI Calladine investigated six months ago feeds into the charge we have Costello on. I would say that the inspector's evidence will be useful but not vital."

"What if Calladine were unable to attend? Would you still get your conviction?"

"Oh yes." Galt smiled. "We have plenty of indisputable forensics, plus testimony from eyewitnesses. Why do you ask?"

Greco sighed. He was going to have to say something. After all, it was highly likely that Calladine wouldn't show up in court. "Calladine has gone missing. Talk has it that Costello has paid him off. Ensured his silence."

"I'd say that was utter rubbish! I can think of at least four others that Costello would like to make disappear before he bothered with Calladine. The man is the old school type of villain. He doesn't pay people off to make them disappear. He has other, more permanent methods, if you get my meaning. You've been misled, DCI Greco."

"You're sure? There is nothing Calladine could add to the proceedings that would ensure Costello got a longer sentence, for example?"

Galt shook his head. "Costello is going down for a long time, with or without Calladine's evidence."

* * *

The Edinburgh train was late. By the time it pulled in, Ruth had been pacing up and down the platform for over half an hour. She was on edge.

Calladine was one of the last off the train. Ruth barely recognised him. He was dishevelled, unshaven, and he couldn't stop yawning. And despite what he'd told her, he still had the angry red shingles rash down one side of his face. Ruth gave him a hug. "Good to have you back. You've no idea how worried we've been."

"Try being me! That was one helluva journey. I had to wait in Inverness for at least two hours to get a connection."

"I'm talking about what happened to you, not the journey home, idiot!" She was in no mood for jokes.

He grinned. "I wasn't best pleased with events myself. Bashed over the head, then taken to some godforsaken spot in northern Scotland. The escape was no picnic either. Threats or no threats they won't get away with it. Have you told Birch?"

"Yes. She is having the place looked at and she's organised round-the-clock protection for Harry and Zoe. You should give Zoe a call, tell her what's happening," Ruth suggested. "I bumped into Jo earlier but I didn't say much. I thought it was better coming from you."

"The sooner those bastards are arrested and locked up, the better. Has Birch said anything to you about how the raid has gone?"

"I've hardly been at the nick today, so she's not had a chance."

"I don't want any mistakes, Ruth. There is a big rough bloke and a woman at that house. They are sure to know who else is involved in this. They could be key to clearing my name."

"In the meantime, we'll work behind the scenes, find out who these people are and what they want."

"The rest of the team?"

"They know you're back, and that's all. I see you have a black eye." A change of subject.

"The other chap has a broken arm," Calladine said with a satisfied smile.

"You're joking!" Bravado, Ruth thought.

"No. I'm not a violent type as you know, but it was life or death. The bastard would have done for me. I lashed out at him with a garden spade. Caught him just above the elbow."

Ruth's eyes were wide. "It sounds as if you were lucky to get out alive. For now, it's safer for everyone if you stay hidden. You're going to Doc Hoyle's. That okay?"

"It'll have to be. Doc Hoyle's will do for now."

They walked towards the car park.

"What is happening with regard to the money?" he asked.

"Greco is on your case, and you know what he's like. Probably won't tell us anything. But I've given him Alice to assist. I've had a word with her, and tried to make her understand how important it is to keep us up to speed. But neither of them was in the office when I got back, so I don't know what he's found out, or who he's spoken to."

"Greco will have me hung out to dry given half a chance." Calladine shook his head. "One hundred grand! Just dumped in my account. Who does that? It can't be that hard to find out where it came from. I mean, who do you know with that sort of money to give away?"

"Odds on, it's a bribe from Costello. Birch is convinced you've done a runner with it."

"That woman has a lot to learn. Costello would have me bumped off rather than give me money."

"We tried to tell her that," Ruth said.

"What about Layla and Zoe? What do they think has happened to me?"

"Layla found the blood on your car. She suspects you're in trouble. We saw Jo today. She's suspicious but thinks it's a work thing. You must ring them. Put their minds at rest."

Calladine nodded.

"I'll take you to Doc Hoyle's and leave you to it. It's been a long day, and I've got a difficult discussion to have with Jake."

Calladine looked at her. "About the threats?"

"No, to move, or not to move. I'll be honest, Tom. I'm torn. I'm concerned that either way it'll do irreparable damage to our relationship. If I insist we stay, he's going to resent me. If I go with him, I'll hate it."

"Do you want to go?" Calladine asked.

"Up until you went missing — no. But now, if they throw you out of the force, then it might make the decision easier. Whether I like the idea of moving south or not, I couldn't stay on without you. I was thinking about going for DI, but what with Harry, I think the stress would be too much."

"They won't throw me out," he said. "Me and Greco might not like each other, but he *is* one of the best. If anyone can clear me, then he can." He looked at her. "Want my job, do you? One little hiccup and you jump into my shoes. Got the measure of you now, DS Bayliss."

Ruth knew he was joking, but the idea of climbing the ladder had suddenly evaporated. She liked things just as they were.

She shook her head. "Having to take the lead with this case we're on now has made me appreciate how difficult your job is."

"Tell me about it." He smiled.

"Do you remember the George Norbury case?" Ruth asked.

Calladine nodded.

"We've got another one, exactly the same. Even down to the pink teddy left at the scene. It's doing my head in. The man is locked up. He can't have done it."

"I never thought he'd killed the other one."

Ruth stopped in her tracks. That was a biggy. Calladine didn't speak much about his past cases, but if there was any doubt about the outcome, he'd sometimes bring them up. As far as she could recall, he'd never once mentioned George Norbury.

"Is that why you suggested the case to Alice as one she might look at?"

"I thought it worth her while. She was hell-bent on raking through my old cases, so why not? I suggested that one and a couple of others I had doubts about."

They climbed into Ruth's car and she pulled out into the rush hour traffic. It was slow going. At this time in the evening, Manchester centre was practically gridlocked.

"Go on, explain. You can't leave it like that. As you said, there was evidence, and the man confessed."

Calladine stared out at the line of cars ahead. "I could be wrong. I didn't work with the evidence much, and I didn't take part in any of the interviews either. They were conducted by DCI Boyd and Jack Andrews. Andrews had his doubts, and spoke to me about them on the QT. No one took much notice of him. He was just a DC, and Boyd the DCI, so his word was law. Boyd wanted the case wrapping up, so that's what happened. It was a long time ago, but I don't recall Andrews complaining openly. He just went along with whatever Boyd wanted. But what bothered me most was that Norbury wasn't the full shilling."

"What part did our new chief super take in all this?" Ruth asked.

"He was in on a couple of interviews."

Ruth glanced at his profile. "If it wasn't Norbury, did you have any other suspects?"

"No. Weeks of investigations, and all we had was Norbury. I know he confessed. He knew some important details, and certain items were found in his flat. But I didn't feel right when Boyd told me they were charging him. Gut instinct. You know how it is when you're working a case."

"Did you voice your doubts?" Ruth asked.

"Not really. I was only involved at the start, and not when they were getting to the nitty-gritty. I was away on a course, so I didn't get to know Norbury like the others did. I looked at the evidence when I got back. The CPS were happy, the rest of the team were happy. I had no choice but to let it go."

"And he was convicted."

He nodded. "The jury's decision was unanimous."

"If he didn't do it, surely he would have said something by now."

"Like I said, the man isn't all there."

Chapter 16

Day 4

Greco sat at Calladine's desk. DCI Birch delivered the news that Vincent Costello was refusing to see him. "I'm sorry, Stephen, but that's how it is."

"Did he give a reason?" Greco asked.

"No, but then he doesn't have to. He'll have his reasons, obviously, and I think we know what they are. He won't want to incriminate himself. After all, he is suspected of bribing a serving police officer. That's a serious charge."

"The warrant came through this morning," Greco said. "The bank has emailed me Calladine's latest statement. The money is there, one hundred grand, but I suspect that there'll be quite a trail before it can be traced back to source. Whether that's Costello or not."

"Well it came from somewhere. If not Costello, then who?" She paused, frowning. "You see the problem, Stephen. There's no one else it possibly could have come from. Calladine has dealt with a lot of villains in his time. Some are inside, some are dead — but that kind of money? And then, of course, there's the tipoff we were given."

"The tipoff that you haven't told me anything about. Will you elaborate now? It might help."

"The information was given to me by a vigilant solicitor," Birch said after a while. "The man is part of the team representing Costello. He overheard a conversation between the villain and the senior partner in his firm. According to him, they were discussing the money and Calladine's testimony. The solicitor thought we should know. Given his position, I didn't question its authenticity."

Greco sighed. "I see. So, as well as everything else, we now have a crooked law firm. I may have to check on this myself. It's puzzling. My contact at the CPS said that Calladine's testimony in court will have little impact on the outcome. The CPS reckons they have plenty of evidence to lock Costello up, with or without Calladine. So why would Costello plot to set him up?"

"You've missed something. I know your reputation, Stephen, but my source is sound. Look harder. It's a helluva lot of money, and it was given to Calladine for a reason. We have it on good authority that it came from Costello." Birch stalked out.

Greco was waiting for a phone call. Leesdon didn't suit him, and he wanted this inquiry to be over. He had called in a favour from a banker friend, a woman he knew from when he worked in Norfolk, and she had promised to find out what she could. At the very least, she'd be able to negotiate her way through the trail of banking red tape he kept getting tangled up in. She would phone him this morning. Then it would all be over.

Alice stood in the doorway. "We should be leaving, sir."

"We aren't going. Costello's refused to see us. I'm waiting for some information that should help. In the meantime, I'm going through the files on Calladine's recent cases to see if anyone involved in any of those could be at the bottom of this."

"Can I help?"

"I'm okay on my own for the moment. Your time would be better spent with the team. You have a nasty murder on your hands, and they are short-handed enough as it is."

* * *

Ruth was poring over everything they had so far, which wasn't much. She couldn't stop thinking about Harry. She'd told the staff at his nursery about the threat. They were reassured by the presence of a uniformed officer. The ideal situation would be for Ruth to take time off and look after Harry herself, but that wasn't possible. The staff were aware of her job and the dangers that came with it.

Then there was what Calladine had told her about the Norbury case. She had to get proof. Even if it was just gut instinct, he was rarely wrong.

She noticed that Alice was back at her desk. "The George Norbury file. Can I have it?"

"What are you thinking?" Alice said.

"There might be something in it that'll help." Ruth didn't want to say too much, not to Alice. But she had discussed it with Rocco. "Would you contact Professor Batho, Alice? See if he has anything else for us."

Alice went off to use the office phone. Ruth pulled up a chair next to Rocco's desk. "We're going to go through this file word by word. There has to be something," she said.

The two of them spent the next hour reading through every single interview and report.

Rocco sat back and shook his head. "If there's something here that might help us, I can't see it."

"What convinced the CPS in the end was Norbury's confession," Ruth said. "He told Ford details, things he couldn't have known about the killing unless he was there. It was decided that Norbury had to have either carried it out himself, or was a bystander, and if so, why not tell them?"

"Perhaps he wanted people to think he was a killer. Some folk crave notoriety."

"Read the profile. Norbury's a typical introvert. Tom didn't think Norbury was the killer-type either."

"With respect to the boss, that's not evidence, is it? Anyway, if Norbury didn't do it, why hasn't he said anything? He's banged up. He has no reason to stay quiet."

"Tom reckons he's not right in the head," Ruth said. "That could be the case. Perhaps Norbury was promised something for taking the rap."

Ruth pointed at a paragraph on the sheet she was reading. "Have you seen this? It's a transcript from one of the interviews. Norbury became upset at one point, and was given a break. On his return, it was noted that he had a bruise on his right cheek. When he was asked about it, he told Boyd that he'd stumbled and hit his head."

"What are you getting at?"

"It might sound a bit far-fetched, Rocco, but do you think he was beaten? Forced to do as he was told?"

"Beaten? That's a big step. If he was, there would have been an outcry. He had his own solicitor, right?"

Ruth sighed. "I suppose so. I'm grasping at straws again."

"We haven't considered the gap yet. That's important," Rocco said. "Why hasn't our mysterious killer struck again in all these years?"

That had been puzzling Ruth too. "We could theorise on that one for weeks, but the alternatives are just as puzzling. If we accept that Norbury was guilty, then who was the current killing down to? How did the new killer know every single detail? We'll go and have a word with Tom. When I met him off the train last night, he was knackered. Now that he knows what we're working on and has had time to think, he may have recalled something we can use."

"Morning coffee at the doc's then?" Rocco smiled.

Ruth gave him a mock frown. "This is work, you know."

"What about Alice?"

"We'll leave her here," she said. "Greco might want something."

"Speaking of which, has he said anything?" Rocco asked.

"No, and I'm not asking. He isn't the easiest man to talk to."

"Anyone wants us, we're going back to the Hobfield," Ruth said to Alice. "You can get me on my mobile."

Just as they were about to leave, Birch called out to her in the corridor.

"I'll see you at the car," Ruth told Rocco.

"Moortop Manse has been visited by the Ullapool police. The place is empty, abandoned is what they said. They will email a report through, but the house looked as if it'd been left in a hurry. Pots in the sink, lights left on, even a television left blaring away in the sitting room," Birch said.

"They got scared when Calladine escaped and scarpered. That's the only explanation, ma'am."

"They will send in forensics next. I'll keep you posted."

* * *

They took Ruth's car to Hopecross.

"Had that chat with Jake yet?" Rocco asked.

"No. By the time I'd got Tom to the doc's it was too late. He'd gone to bed. Sulking, I reckon."

"And you? Made up your mind?"

"I'm staying. Tom assures me he'll be back. That'll do for me."

They pulled into the drive of a huge stone house. "Wow," said Rocco. "The old doc lives in some splendour, doesn't he?"

"Haven't you been here before?"

Rocco shook his head.

"It's a lovely property, with great views over the valley. It's just a shame he lives here all on his own."

"Wonder if he wants a lodger?" Rocco mused.

"Why? Are you looking for somewhere? I thought you were settled in that flat overlooking the canal."

"The flat is great," Rocco said, "and the location's perfect. It's just too expensive. The rent is top whack, and there's a service charge as well. If I had someone to share the expenses, it might be different. But as it is, I need a cheaper option."

"Think carefully before you give up your independence, Rocco."

The doc opened the door and smiled at them. "Come to check on our friend? I can report that he ate a hearty meal and had a good night's sleep. I just wish I could get him off the damn computer."

"What's he doing?" Ruth asked.

"Researching that house he was taken to. Reckons he's found it on the map. Come in."

"Moortop Manse," Calladine said by way of a greeting. "Bloody place. Might look good but it's nothing but a fancy prison."

He was studying Google Maps, looking at the road he'd driven down.

Rocco peered over his shoulder. "It's narrow with some sharp bends, and no lighting either. You were lucky to get back in one piece."

"You're keeping my safe return quiet, aren't you?"

Rocco nodded. "What I don't understand is why."

"Threats have been made against our families," Ruth told him. "Harry in particular."

"Us four can know, but no one else," Calladine said.

"Alice isn't daft. She'll want to know why we're holding back."

"Tell her that they got me once, and there's no guaranteeing they won't try again. Explain that things are happening in the background but my reappearance is not for discussion at the nick. I don't want her telling Greco."

Ruth patted his back. "We haven't told a soul."

Rocco was studying the map on the screen. "It's in an isolated spot. If you hadn't escaped, we'd never have found you. You were damn lucky."

"What? That they didn't kill me?" Calladine gave a caustic laugh. "Well, I have no reason to think that they wouldn't have."

"And you have no idea who they were, or who wanted you out of the way?" asked Rocco.

Calladine shook his head. "There it is." He pointed to a large house standing well back from the road. "There's a track, but the map doesn't follow it. The next thing is to find out who owns the damn place. I'll get on with that later."

"Whoever they were, they've done a runner," Ruth told him. "The Ullapool police raided but the place was empty."

Calladine swung the chair round. "They must be rattled."

"Have you spoken to Zoe?"

"Yes. Her and Jo have taken an impromptu holiday. They won't even tell me where they've gone. I've to text when everything is sorted and the danger has passed."

"Layla is worried too," Ruth reminded him.

"I'll ring her later."

"We want to ask you about the George Norbury case," Rocco said. "We have a copycat on our hands, but we've no idea where he got the details from."

"Ford, Jack Andrews, the pathologist or SOCO team at the time, or from me. Anyone of us could have said something. Talked about the case in the pub, to friends or family."

"You didn't." Ruth smiled.

"No, I never do. Once a case is wrapped up and filed away, that's it. Speaking of which, have you checked who's had access to the case file? That could be your answer."

"It languished untouched in the archive until Alice took it out last week." Ruth said. "Yesterday you hinted you had doubts about Norbury's guilt. That could be our answer. It wasn't Norbury at all but a different killer, someone who's got a taste for it again."

"I have no proof of that, only my doubts from years ago. Look at the interviews, what Norbury said." Calladine paused. "I know Angus Ford is now our chief super, but he did work the case. It wouldn't do any harm to have a chat with him about it. He has no reason to refuse. I would also try a bit harder to find Boyd and Andrews. Both were local. Andrews came to us straight from university."

"Like Alice?" Ruth said.

Calladine nodded. "But unlike Alice, his degree wasn't in criminology as I recall."

"What did he major in?"

He shrugged. "Can't remember. It was a while ago."

The doc had disappeared to take a phone call. He returned, looking flustered. "I've been asked to go in. I'm still doing the locum thing. This time it's Leesdon Infirmary. They're chock-full. I'll have to leave you folks to it."

Calladine looked at Ruth. "Have that conversation with Ford. I'll find out who owns Moortop Manse, and we'll talk later."

Chapter 17

"DCI Birch is looking for you," Alice said when Ruth returned.

"I'll go and see what she wants. Did you get anything from Julian?"

"The forensic artist is coming to see you later. He's done a couple of sketches."

Ruth hurried along the corridor to Birch's office. The DCI probably wanted an update on the case. The truth was, they didn't have much. She'd have to be careful how she put it. Keep it upbeat. The alternative was having Long take charge.

"DS Bayliss. Come in," Birch said in her best official voice.

After a quick glance at the man sitting with her, Ruth knew why Birch sounded so serious. She'd never met him in person, but Ruth had seen his photo. It was the new chief super, Angus Ford. Birch was all smiles. Not a good sign.

"Given that DI Calladine is indisposed, I have been telling DCS Ford that it has fallen to you to organise the team. How are you doing?"

"We are making progress, ma'am."

"Do you have the victim's identity yet?"

"I'm hopeful we'll have it later today." Not a yes, but not a straight no either. If the forensic artist failed to produce a likeness that someone recognised, they were scuppered.

"This is Detective Chief Superintendent Ford. As you know, he now has responsibility for the Leesdon and Oldston stations."

The two exchanged nods. "Actually, sir, I was going to ask to speak to you about our current case." Ruth saw Birch frown.

"You think I can help?" He turned and looked straight at Ruth, seeming to notice her for the first time.

Ruth felt nervous under his scrutiny. She had not been asked to sit down, and was standing awkwardly beside the desk.

Ford was about Calladine's age, but that was where the likeness ended. Ford was tall, thin and balding, with a florid face. His most striking feature was his long nose. He did not look a fit man. Stress was a killer in this job, and Ford appeared to have had his fair share. She guessed he was someone who lived on his nerves.

"A number of years ago, sir, you worked on the George Norbury case."

His face turned a deeper red. "Yes, I did. Why do you ask?"

"Your knowledge of that case may help us, sir."

"I doubt it. It was a long time ago and the perpetrator is locked up. You would do better to concentrate on your current case load. Looking back will get you nowhere."

But Ruth was not to be put off. "This time it might, sir. You see, the murder we are currently investigating has exactly the same MO as the Norbury killing. Hardly a coincidence."

Ford's eyes narrowed and he pursed his lips. He evidently wasn't happy at being asked the question.

His tone was measured. "Of course I'll help in any way I can. But you have to know that my input was minimal. What exactly are you suggesting?"

"Just that it's an odd coincidence, sir."

"Might I suggest that that is exactly what it is. What is on your mind, Sergeant? Do you think we put the wrong man away?"

"I'm not suggesting anything, sir. The facts speak for themselves. Our current case is similar to that one in almost every detail. And that's odd, given that the details of the Norbury case weren't publicised."

"You did not work that case, Sergeant. If you had seen the evidence, listened to Norbury's confession, you would have no doubts. DCI Boyd and the team listened to hours of gruesome details related by Norbury." He shook his head. "The man is evil. Given that Calladine isn't here, how did you find out about this similarity?"

Ruth found his question odd. What did it matter? Ford was staring at her. He had large, piercing brown eyes. Why did she feel that she'd done wrong to discover the similarity? Then she remembered that if it hadn't been for Alice poking around in the archive, they would never have become aware of the connection. As Ford had pointed out, Calladine was absent, and it was before Julian's time. It had been Alice who had alerted them.

"We have a new recruit in the team who's very sharp," Ruth said. "She's been looking through a number of DI Calladine's old cases. She was studying the George Norbury file when the body was discovered and spotted the similarities immediately."

"Rest assured, Sergeant, there was no mistake! Norbury was as guilty as sin. I know that better than anyone. I saw the evidence, read the man's statements, and listened to him relate the sick details. After that, we did everyone a favour and put him away."

"Given the similarities, sir, I would be failing in my duty if I didn't ask."

"Your tone suggests that you think we may have been wrong, Sergeant. You should think twice before you question the judgement of your superiors in cases you were not party to." He paused, his breathing slightly laboured. "Norbury, or someone else connected to the case, has told someone. That's your answer."

Calladine had said the same thing. "I was simply asking if you could suggest anything, sir. We are working flat out, against the clock. There is no guarantee that the killer won't strike again."

"I can't help. You are wasting your time with the Norbury angle. Look elsewhere. Do not waste valuable resources going over old ground."

He sounded calmer, but Ruth could see that Ford was struggling to regain his composure. His irritation at being questioned was evident on his face. Even his eyes were red. God knows what it must have been like to be part of his team. The man had a volatile temper. Was it just this particular case? Or did he react like this every time he was asked about an old one?

"After the first few interviews, Norbury confessed in glorious technicolour to anyone who would listen. Alternatively, anyone connected with that case could have let details slip. Calladine himself, for example. What you have, Sergeant, is a copycat killing." He sat back in his chair.

Ruth didn't dare contradict the man for fear of provoking him any further. But that wasn't Calladine's take on the case. He'd told her that Norbury did know things, but it was only after they'd found evidence at his home that he confessed.

* * *

So much for having a chat with the new boss. All Ruth had done was alienate him. He definitely wasn't pleased at what she'd said. But Ruth couldn't understand why. She put it down to ego. The man thought that because he was the boss, he always had to be right. She'd just wanted his help. She hadn't been criticising him, but that was how he'd seen it.

Ruth was still shaken when she got back to the incident room. Ford had a bad temper and was no doubt a bully too. They'd get no help from him, that was for sure.

"Michael!" The forensic artist had arrived and was chatting to Rocco. His friendly smile cheered her up immediately.

"What did Birch want? On our backs, is she?" asked Rocco.

"She had the new super with her. Tom was right, he's a bad-tempered old bugger. I spoke to him about the case, but he was no help at all. In fact, he took the fact that I'd asked him about it as a personal attack."

"The boss doesn't like him much either," Rocco said.

"That's not the point though, is it? He led the investigation. He should offer us his support, not take offence!"

Michael held out a sheaf of papers. "I've done one or two sketches. Difficult because of the mouth, but they might help."

Ruth looked at them carefully. "Rocco, have you seen these?"

"No, I was waiting for you."

"This one, who does it remind you of? I'd go as far as to say we've seen her very recently. Or someone who looks very like her."

Rocco took it from her. "That girl, the edgy one in Heron House! The one who didn't want to talk. That sketch is the spit of her."

"That has to be more than coincidence. We'll get back there, show her this and see if she feels more like talking to us now," Ruth said.

* * *

"You should tell the boss about Ford's reluctance to help," Rocco suggested as they drove.

"I don't understand the man," she said. "Calladine did express his doubts about Norbury's guilt. I wonder if he voiced them to Ford? That could be why they don't get on."

They pulled up in front of Heron House. "We're in luck. She's over there, see?" Rocco pointed at a young woman with a pushchair.

Ruth got out of the car. "Come on. Let's see if we can get the truth out of her this time."

"Ingrid Plesec!" she called. "We'd like a word."

"I've already told you. I don't know anything." The girl gripped the pushchair handles so tight that her knuckles were pale.

"You don't know what we want yet." Ruth took one of the sketches from her bag. "Do you know this woman?"

The girl was shaking. She glanced at the image and immediately turned her eyes away. She shook her head.

"I think you do know her. Look again." Ruth pushed the page in front of her. "You are very alike. In fact, with a little tweak here and there, this could be you."

The young woman burst into tears. "She's my sister."

"Do you know where she is?" Ruth asked.

"No. I haven't seen her in weeks. She's in trouble, isn't she? I knew Ingrid would drag me into something sooner or later."

The young woman was really upset. They should be sitting down somewhere. "Is there anywhere we can talk?" Ruth asked.

"Tell me now. Here." The girl pulled herself up to her full height.

"You said Ingrid?" Ruth said, puzzled. "I thought that was your name. Would you like to explain?"

"Ingrid disappeared. Ran away, I think. We'd had an argument about her behaviour, particularly the way she treated Lara."

"Was it a bad one? Did you come to blows?"

She shook her head. "No, nothing like that."

"So why didn't you tell us she was missing?" Ruth asked.

"We lived together but everything we have is in Ingrid's name. The flat, the bank account, all the state benefits for Lara." She smiled down at the sleeping child in the pushchair.

Ruth knew at once what she'd done. "So, Ingrid goes missing and you take her identity?"

"What else could I do? I had to look after Lara."

"You could have come to us. Told the truth about what happened." Ruth had a bad feeling about this. Whatever the truth about the Norbury killing, an argument between the sisters might be a motive for murder.

"I'm sorry. I know that now. I am Alenka Plesec, not Ingrid. Please don't be angry. I only wanted to make sure Lara was safe till Ingrid came home. She will one day, I know it."

"I'm afraid we have bad news, Alenka. We believe your sister is dead."

Tears began running down Alenka's face. "How did she die? What happened to her, an accident?"

"We need to talk to you properly, down at the station. Is there someone who can look after the child for you?" Ruth said. She didn't want to cause a scene out here. Telling the young woman that her sister had been murdered was a dreadful task.

"There is a woman, flat three on the ground floor. I can ask her."

Ruth's mobile rang. It was Calladine.

"Have you seen the local rag?"

"No, sorry, too busy working. Why, what rubbish have they printed now?"

"You need to get a copy. They've reported on your victim. The details are all there, including the soft toy and the branding. You've got to stop anything further from being leaked. If you're not careful, it'll start a panic."

"What can we do? It's out there now."

"For starters, you can find out who told them."

Chapter 18

He had been watching her for days. Her routine rarely varied. She also had a partner who worked nights, which was a bonus. No one to ask those awkward questions, or ring the police when she didn't come home.

He'd watched enough. It was necessary, but boring. Now it was time to strike.

The evening was cold, darkness falling fast. The hospital car park was unsheltered, and a stiff breeze was blowing. He turned up his overcoat collar and made his move.

"It'll rain before much longer. This wind keeps up, it'll be a bad night." He smiled. It was meant to sound like a friendly comment from a fellow visitor. But she looked straight ahead. "When does visiting time end?"

"Seven, I think," she said. "I'm not sure. I'm not visiting. I work here. Now I'm off home."

"You know the area? In that case, perhaps you can help me. I've come to see a relative but I don't live round here. Do you know how I get back to the M62?"

"There are signs at the main roundabout as you leave town. You need to go towards Oldston."

"Oldston?"

Now she looked at him. She was young, but her face was drawn and tired. "Use a satnav or something."

Her irritation was understandable, he supposed. She probably thought he was being pushy, but it annoyed him nevertheless. He'd have to work quickly, or she'd be gone. "Perhaps I could give you a lift, and then you can show me."

"Who are you? What do you want?" Her eyes narrowed.

"Like I said, I've been visiting a relative. But I have a distance to travel and want to make sure I take the right road." He watched her face. She was considering this. It was spitting with rain and she only had a thin jacket on. A lift would be too tempting to refuse.

"Which ward is your relative on?" she asked.

Checking his story, he guessed. Well, he'd done his homework. He pointed. "Ward G4, in that block over there. Heart surgery."

"Okay. You can drop me at the top of our street. It's not far into Oldston from there."

Success! He unlocked the car and she slid into the passenger seat beside him. She smelled of disinfectant and soap, and was wearing a green overall under the jacket. He'd assumed she was a nurse. But still, it made no difference to the end result.

She'd seen him looking. She frowned. "I'm a cleaner. Someone has to do it, don't they?"

He started the engine and pulled out of the car park. Out on the road, she prattled on about the one-way system. Excited, anticipating the kill, he didn't listen.

"I'll pull into that layby coming up ahead. You can show me on the map," he said.

She was looking away from him, staring out of the window at the rain. Easy. She wouldn't know what hit her. He reached down beside him, took hold of the claw hammer and with a single hefty swipe, caught her on the temple. The blow knocked her out cold.

* * *

"We can't ask Alenka to identify the body," Ruth said. "It would be too traumatic. The face has been mutilated and there is the decomposition. We have to think of something else."

"We could have a word with the morgue. Perhaps they could cover the lower part of the face. Ask the young woman about the birthmark with the tattoo. She'll know about that, surely?" Rocco said.

Ruth smiled. "Good thinking, Rocco. She's in an interview room. We'll have a word shortly."

It was getting late. Alice and Joyce had already left. Ruth didn't want to stay — it meant Jake having to see to Harry again. But she had to speak to Alenka tonight.

Rhona Birch entered the incident room. Despite her smile, her voice had an edge to it. "Breakthrough, I believe?"

"Yes, ma'am. We have a possible identity."

"And a suspect too?"

"We have the victim's sister, but I doubt she's our killer. We've brought her in for interview, and to make a statement. She may be able to help us with the details of Ingrid's life, especially the night she went missing."

Birch's smile had vanished. "Superintendent Ford was not pleased with you questioning him like that."

"I would hardly call it questioning, ma'am. I didn't get the chance. If you don't mind me asking, why is he so reluctant to discuss the Norbury case?"

"He's convinced the team got the right man. Simple as that. Ford is a thorough investigator, an excellent policeman. He got results in his time, people thought highly of him. The Norbury case isn't the only one he's sensitive about. He puts people away. Like you and the team here, he sees what killers do. When he gets a result, and the CPS agree with the evidence, he considers his job done. He doesn't look back, and he doesn't expect his colleagues to do so either."

"He was angry, ma'am."

"It's just his way." Her tone was softer now. "He's a volatile man, it's true, and he does have a temper. I'm sure DI Calladine, if he ever returns, will be only too quick to tell you that."

Ruth wasn't unconvinced. After her interview with Ford, she was certain that the Norbury issue was about something else entirely. But Birch was already on her way to the door.

"Want to do this now?" Rocco asked.

She grabbed the case file. "Let's get on with it. It's getting late. I was going to see Tom after work, but I'd better get off home or Jake'll think I've dumped him. And I need to see to Harry. I've been worrying myself sick about him all day."

Rocco smiled. "I can pop round if you like. See what the boss's turned up on that house he was kept in."

"You really do fancy becoming the doc's lodger, don't you?"

Rocco shrugged. "Can't be much fun living all the way out there on his own."

"Tread carefully. The doc is great and all that, but living with him would be a different matter. He's been on his own for years."

"I've got to do something, Ruth. The rent on that flat is crippling me."

* * *

Alenka Plesec was still tearful. "Am I in trouble?"

"You've been masquerading as your sister. Drawing benefits in her name, for a start. I'd imagine that the DWP will want a word." Ruth opened the file. "But for now, I want you to think about the day Ingrid went out and didn't come back. Do you know where she went?"

"Not exactly. But I know she had a cleaning job."

"Was this a regular job?" Rocco asked.

"No. Ingrid wanted to start her own business. She put notices up in shop windows and advertised online. She used her mobile number for that. It was early January, just after Christmas. She got a call and said she'd have to go out."

"Did she say who rang her, or where she was going?"

Alenka Plesec burst into tears all over again. "I didn't ask. I was angry with her and we had an argument. I was supposed to go out to my night class, but I couldn't because I was worried about Lara. Ingrid said just to leave her. I couldn't do that. I shouted at her — she never took responsibility for the child. By the time Ingrid left the flat, we weren't speaking."

"Did you hear the phone conversation?" Ruth asked.

"Not really, but I know it was a man. Ingrid was pleased. Apparently he said that his wife was away and he needed a big clean-up after Christmas. He promised her a hundred pounds."

That would certainly tempt a hard-up young woman. "And she didn't return that night?"

Alenka shook her head.

"Can you tell me if Ingrid had any distinguishing marks?" Ruth said.

Alenka looked puzzled.

"Did she have any birthmarks or moles?"

"She has a heart shape on the nape of her neck," Alenka said. "A friend of ours tattooed an outline around it. But you can't see it now that Ingrid wears her hair long."

"Would you be prepared to take a look at the body? It would firm things up for us."

"Yes, of course."

"I must warn you that it won't be easy. She has been dead for several weeks and her mouth was mutilated."

"If it's Ingrid, then I'll know."

"One of our officers will take you to the morgue. A few seconds that's all it will take. How old was Ingrid?"

"Twenty-three."

Chapter 19

Day 5

John Robbins had booked his car in for its MOT. The garage he used was on a side street off the bypass, in one of a number of old railway arches that had long since been converted into industrial units. A variety of businesses operated from here. Besides the garage, there was a joinery and a small firm that did sheet-metal work. The end unit was empty. The 'to let' sign had been there so long it was peppered with holes and barely legible. As he pulled up, Robbins saw that the old double doors were swinging in the breeze. Someone had broken in.

It was early, and the garage wasn't open yet. Robbins got out of his car and went for a look around. The empty unit at the end intrigued him. Years ago when he'd been a child, these railway arches were empty, and were great places to play in. He and his mates had spent many a wet afternoon inside them, building dens and playing hide and seek.

Inside, the air was damp and cold. There was no lighting, the corners all in shadow. These days the place would be a refuge for the homeless. Perhaps it was one of them who'd left the doors open this morning.

He took a last look, turned to go and then stopped. Something dark, smeared across the concrete, had caught his eye. Over to his right, by the wall, he saw a trail of fresh blood leading off into the corner. He squinted into the gloom. It looked as if someone had been injured and then dragged further into the arch. He called out. There could be someone lying hurt back there, unable to help themselves. Drug taking was rife among the homeless. Perhaps there'd been a fight. But there was no reply to his call. He took a few hesitant steps further inside. He'd no idea what was lurking in the gloom. He got as far as an old workbench about halfway in, when he stopped and gasped.

A young woman, her blank eyes staring into nothing. Her throat had been cut. For a few seconds Robbins was transfixed. He'd never even seen a dead body before. And this wasn't just a dead body, this was a murder victim he was looking at, had to be. The sight was horrific. She was nailed to something and things had been done to her. Robin gagged, then dashed outside and threw up. Then he phoned the police.

* * *

"It's the same as the last one," Rocco said.

"Except that she's only been dead since last night," Ruth pointed out. "That'll be helpful. Forensics are fresh. No decay."

"She was nailed to that upright beam in there. Naked, branded, and he slit her throat."

"What about the teddy?" Ruth asked. "CSI found any sign?"

"He left it wedged in one of her hands, just like the others."

Ruth pushed back a stray lock of hair from her face. They badly needed a break. Another body meant that

Birch was bound to assign Long's team to the case. Brilliant!

A CSI officer called to her. "We're going to move the body out now."

Natasha Barrington came across and stood with Ruth and Rocco. "I'll do the PM right away. At first sight it looks very like the last one."

"Do we know who she is?" asked Ruth.

Natasha shook her head. "Not yet. But the PM might give us something."

Ruth's mobile rang. Calladine.

"We're up to our eyes in it," she said before he had time to speak. "We need you back, Tom. We've got another body, same as before. Isn't there anything you can do to put this right? Prove your innocence?"

"That's in Greco's hands."

"I'll have a word when I get back to the nick. In the meantime, will you think carefully about the Norbury case? There has to be some connection with what's happening now."

"What did Ford say?" Calladine asked.

"He took my questions as a personal attack on him. He lost his cool and told me I was wrong."

"I want you to do something for me. I've traced the owners of Moortop Manse, but I'm no closer. It's owned by a firm I've never heard of."

Just then, Rocco called out to her. "Tom, I've got to go. Text me the name, and I'll look them up on the system, see if anything is known about them." As if she didn't have enough to do!

"And don't say anything to Greco. I've got a little surprise for him."

Ruth walked away from a uniform standing too close to her. "Don't do anything stupid, Tom! We need you on the case, but go upsetting everyone and it'll be weeks before you're back."

"Trust me. I know what I'm doing."

* * *

"My mind is made up, Doc. I can't kick my heels around yours forever." Calladine poured himself another mug of coffee. "Don't think I'm not grateful, because I am. But there's a job to be done, and now that a second body has been found, the team'll be struggling."

"That isn't good, I agree. But you've been suspended. Don't forget, investigations are still ongoing regarding the corruption allegations against you. There's not a lot you can do about the murders right now."

Calladine set down his mug hard, spilling coffee. "I've done nowt wrong! I was kidnapped! Given half a chance to speak up, Birch, Ford and company would see that. This is a bloody stupid state of affairs. If things had moved faster the buggers would be locked up tight."

"Calm down. I'm sure Ruth'll keep you up to date with the state of play."

"She'll be run off her feet. She's at the crime scene now. From what she said, it's the same MO as before. I need to be there. See the evidence, talk to the witnesses first hand."

"Do you know who owns that house you were taken to?" Doc Hoyle asked.

"Some organisation whose name I don't know. I haven't got any further. Next thing is to find out what they do."

"Simple enough job, Tom. If it's a limited company, an internet search will give you the names of the directors."

"I'll work on that later. For now my head is full of job stuff. I can see Ruth now, doing her scalded cat impression, Birch snapping at her heels, wailing for results. I can't sit by and let the team suffer."

Calladine went upstairs to change, leaving Doc Hoyle staring after him. Ten minutes later he reappeared, wearing a suit, complete with shirt and tie.

The doc smiled. "DCI Birch is not that impressionable. You might look good, but she's a hard nut."

"It's not her I'm going to see. I want a word with Greco."

Chapter 20

Jackie Lomax, Greco's banker friend, got back to him that morning. "It's good to hear from you, Stephen. We've missed you." She laughed. "Quiz nights in the 'Boatman' are just not the same. I read in the papers what happened to Suzy. I am sorry, Stephen. You must have been devastated."

"I was." His tone ruled out further talk on the matter. "What have you got for me?"

"The money has led me a merry dance, I can tell you. It was transferred several times, from bank to bank. A couple of them were offshore."

"Someone did want to cover their tracks?"

"Up to a point. But with patience and the right access, it wasn't impossible to unravel the trail. The money originated from a company called 'Heights Industrial.' Ever heard of them?"

"Never. Could you find any connection at all to one Vincent Costello?"

"Nothing, Stephen. And I did a thorough search. The money has gone nowhere near him, nor any organisation he is, or has ever been, involved with."

That was good news for Calladine. "Thanks, Jackie. I owe you a favour."

Greco replaced the receiver and at once the phone rang again.

"Can we meet?"

"DI Calladine?" Tom Calladine was the last person he expected to hear from. "Where are you?"

"Near enough."

"Do you know what's been going on? Where did you disappear to?"

"I don't want to talk over the phone. There's a café behind the bus station in Leesdon. Meet me there in half an hour. Don't tell anyone. We need to talk."

Greco wrote the name 'Heights Industrial' on a notepad he kept in his jacket pocket. He would keep the rendezvous. He had no idea what was going on, but after the call from Jackie Lomas, he was certain that Tom Calladine hadn't taken a bribe, or disappeared out of choice.

* * *

Greco found Calladine sitting in a window seat facing the bus station, sipping coffee.

"If you've not had breakfast, I recommend the full English. Otherwise, stick to tea or coffee. The rest of the food they serve up here leaves a lot to be desired," Calladine told Greco.

Greco went to the counter, ordered a coffee and sat down opposite Calladine. "You do know that I'm investigating your disappearance and what happened to you?"

Calladine nodded. "Just as well we've met up then. I can save you a lot of work."

"I shouldn't tell you this," Greco said, "but rumour has it you took a bribe from Costello, then dropped out of sight of your own accord."

"That's rubbish."

Greco looked straight at him. "Given what I learned during the last hour, I think you're right."

This came as a surprise. He hadn't expected Greco to be so easily convinced. After all, the two of them had history. Greco disliked him. "You've found something?"

"I've traced the money that made its way into your account. It didn't come from Costello. I've had a thorough look at your cases over the last year or so and I can find no reason why anyone involved in them would want to bribe you."

This was real progress. "I was kidnapped. Hit on the head and taken from outside my house. I'm likely to have a scar on the back of my head to prove it. When I came to, I was in a strange, old house up in the north of Scotland."

Greco stared at him. "When you escaped why didn't you tell the police straight away? Ullapool is remote but there is a force up there."

"I fully intended to, but there were complications." He paused. "Threats were made against our families, against Ruth's son, Harry."

Greco was still staring. "Nonetheless, you should have come straight in. You have a black eye."

"Getting free was tricky."

"Can you think of anyone who would want you out of the way?" Greco asked.

"No, and believe me, I've thought of little else these past days."

"Does the name 'Heights Industrial' mean anything to you?" Greco said.

Calladine was taken aback. He reached in his overcoat pocket for his notebook. "Yes. It's the name of the organisation that owns the house I was taken to — Moortop Manse."

"Snap!" Greco produced his own notebook. "It's the same firm that put the money in your account."

"Do you know who they are? Where they operate from?" Now they were getting to it. Calladine was fired up now, and raring to go.

"Not yet. I was only given the name this morning, moments before you called, in fact."

"Birch doesn't know?" Calladine asked.

"No," said Greco. "When I get back to the station, do I bring her up to date? I take it the threat still stands. Sergeant Bayliss must be scared witless. I know I would be if someone threatened my child."

"Harry has a uniformed officer watching him. My daughter has disappeared with her partner and told no one. I have to return to work. My team have a tricky case on their hands, and they need me."

Greco frowned. "You're quite right. You are a serving policeman. You were kidnapped. That in itself is a major crime. Add to that the recent threats and we are looking for some dangerous people."

"You agree then. I re-join my team."

"Where are you staying?" Greco asked.

"With Dr Hoyle in Hopecross village."

"I'll speak to Birch. Go back to Hopecross and wait there until I ring you."

"What made Birch and them upstairs believe I'd taken Costello's money in the first place?" Calladine said.

"A tip-off."

"And that's all it took to condemn me as a bloody criminal!" Calladine was dumbfounded. "All the years I've given to the job! Suddenly they count for bugger all."

"Ford asked me to carry out the initial investigation and to determine if the case should be taken further. He could have passed it onto the anti-corruption squad, but he didn't. In my opinion, that isn't condemning you out of hand," Greco said.

"I've worked with Ford. Knowing him as I do, that only makes me trust him even less. Where did this tip-off come from?"

"A solicitor on Costello's team gave the information to Birch. I've tried to contact him without success. I've spoken to the head of the firm and he denies all knowledge of it. Birch then passed the information on to Ford. They'll have discussed it. Whether they got any further than I did trying to validate it is another matter, but both Birch and Ford were convinced. But they wouldn't divulge who it came from, except to say that it was a source they trust absolutely.

Calladine gave a humourless laugh. "They'll know better in future then, won't they?"

* * *

Greco returned to the station. The Calladine case was dragging on longer than he'd hoped. Now he had proved that the DI hadn't taken a bribe, Birch and Ford would want to know who had kidnapped him and why. With any luck, they'd let Calladine himself get on with that one.

Greco went to see Birch.

"You met with Calladine alone?" she said. "That wasn't wise. You should have told me. Are you sure that there's no mistake about what you discovered? Costello's a seasoned villain. He knows how to cover his tracks."

"There is no mistake. Costello might know all the tricks, but Calladine was taken for some other reason, and whatever that is, it isn't connected to Costello. Calladine was attacked outside his home and imprisoned in a house in the north of Scotland. You are protecting those they threatened, but he may still be at risk. These people are ruthless."

The look she gave him could have frozen the sea. "The child, I agree, but I do not have the resources to guard Calladine twenty-four/seven."

"He wants to return to duty. Given what we now know, I see no reason why he shouldn't."

Birch heaved a sigh. "I'll get onto the Scottish police ask if forensics have found anything. I'll tell Ford what you've discovered. Uniform will keep an eye on Calladine and his house."

"Thank you. I'll be returning to my own station tomorrow."

Chapter 21

Calladine reluctantly went back to Doc Hoyle's house. The meeting with Greco had gone better than he'd expected, but he still needed to get back to work. Greco had promised to speak to Birch and Ford. It was something, but would it bear fruit? Calladine had been racking his brain as to why the kidnappers had chosen him. It had to be connected with something he was working on, but he couldn't for the life of him think what.

He started researching Heights Industrial. There was very little. The company was newly formed, and the directors' names meant nothing to him. He would have to use the resources back at the nick to get any further.

"The hospital has been on again. They want me back in. As if last night wasn't bad enough," Doc Hoyle complained. "I've only had four hours' sleep. They forget how old I am."

"Busy night?" Calladine asked.

"Busy doesn't cut it, Tom. It's been bloody manic. A&E is chock-full with kids who've all taken something new. Some sort of cheap designer drug has hit the streets. No one knows anything about it: who's supplying it or who's manufacturing it. It was a close run thing with one young girl. She's damn lucky to be alive."

"All local?" Calladine asked.

"We had Oldston and the big hospital at Trafford Park on, asking for advice. Leesdon has a specialist drugs unit. They had a spate of the same thing too."

That meant there was probably a new supplier in the area, someone who'd spread his wings wide. "Did you manage to get your hands on any of it?" Calladine asked.

"Yes. Pills. They're in the lab being analysed now." The doc took his mobile from his pocket and showed Calladine a photo. "See what I mean? Proper pills, blue ones, in tiny see-through plastic bags each holding about five."

Calladine peered at the image.

"Dr Hampson says they're methamphetamines," the doc said. "Street name's speed or meth. But they're not like the usual stuff. These pills were professionally produced. Someone out there has got an illegal lab and a production line going."

Calladine frowned. More work. Leesdon station would have to investigate their share of this. Ruth would be tearing her hair out.

"Anything else, apart from the meth?" he asked.

"A couple of homeless people had taken too much spice. They've been sleeping rough in the underpass by the motorway. As you'd expect, there were more of those in Trafford Park than around here. We got a sample. Same packaging, so we suspect the same firm, Tom."

Calladine knew what that meant. Some bright spark with the knowhow and the contacts had gone into business for himself. But who? "Any of them talk to you? Say who they bought it off?"

Doc Hoyle shook his head. "No way. You know what it's like, Tom. Talk, and they believe they're dead meat. There must be quite a setup somewhere out there. It will have taken a great deal of organising and financial investment. Also, there'll be waste. Production, on the scale we're seeing, will create a lot of it. It's dangerous and needs disposing of correctly."

Calladine decided to ring Ruth and find out what the teams at the nick were doing about it. He was right. She wasn't happy.

"Drugs! We haven't got the time. We're up to our eyes in it with the two murders. There was a briefing about the drug issue this morning. Birch has allocated that investigation to Long, which suits me no end. It gets him off our backs. I was terrified he'd be given our case in your absence."

"About that," Calladine said. "I met Greco this morning."

Ruth laughed. "I'd like to have been a fly on the wall at that one."

"He was okay actually, very reasonable. He knows I'm innocent and he can prove it. Once he sorts it with Birch and Ford, I should be back. Ford didn't pass my alleged misdemeanour upstairs for investigation, which is something to be grateful for. He wanted Greco's take on things first."

"With Greco's endorsement, you should be back soon then?" Ruth asked.

"Tomorrow hopefully."

"Greco is back in his office," she said, "or rather your office. He's been on the phone a lot, but he hasn't said anything to us. I'll let you know the moment we get told what's happening about you."

So, Long was investigating the drug problem, was he? It might keep him out of Ruth's hair, but that was about it. Whoever was at the bottom of it would run rings around the man.

The doc had given Calladine plenty to think about. He picked up the phone again and rang Eve Buckley. She might be able to advise him on where the waste from such an operation would be taken for disposal. The Buckley family owned a pharmaceutical company in Leesworth that employed half the adults in the area.

Although Eve Buckley was his birth mother, she hadn't raised him. Calladine was the product of an affair between Eve and Calladine's father, Frank. Eve Walker, as she had been then, hadn't been able to cope. She was young, unable to support herself. Her horrified parents had told her to put the infant up for adoption. Eve hadn't wanted that, so she asked Frank for help. He took the newborn infant home to his wife, Freda. Unable to have children of her own, she accepted him, and raised him as her own son. Calladine could not recall his parents ever discussing this, nor did Eve ever come looking. It was only after the deaths of Frank and then Freda that he learned that the three of them had agreed this plan. Calladine had only learned the truth about his family fairly recently, when Freda had died. Although he was gradually getting used to the idea of Eve, he didn't think of her as his mother. But she was a reality, and lived nearby. She had two other children, Samantha and Simon, his half-brother and sister.

Eve was not at home when he phoned. Her housekeeper told him that she'd gone into Manchester. He left a message. They would speak later.

* * *

"I can take Alice along if you'd rather," Ruth said.

"No, I'm fine. Don't get me wrong. It's true I hate going to PMs," Rocco said. "All that blood and cutting up isn't pleasant, but it's all part of the job." He gathered up his things, ready to leave.

"Fortunately for us, Natasha has nothing else on, so she can do this one now," Ruth said.

"Poor lass, whoever she was. I told you there'd be more."

Ruth hadn't seriously considered it, because the first body had gone so long undiscovered. She should have. "Alice, would you have a trawl through the recent missing person reports while we're gone? You never know, we might strike lucky. Now that Alenka has identified her sister's body we need Ingrid Plesec's phone records too. Get on to the provider, will you?"

Alice nodded. "Knowing the number that offer of work came from might help. But what's the betting it's an unregistered mobile?"

"Got to try, nonetheless," Rocco said.

On their way out, Ruth cast a glance Greco's way. He was still closeted in Calladine's office, phone in hand.

"Things are looking better for Tom. Turns out Greco believes he's innocent too."

Rocco frowned. "But who put the money in the boss's account then? Has he answered that one yet?"

"Tom is looking into that. But the dosh definitely didn't come from Costello. That means he's in the clear. Someone is obviously trying to frame him."

Traffic was light, and soon they were in the Duggan Centre, mounting the steps to the viewing platform. Ruth sighed. "Twice in one week, Rocco. Grim, and tragic."

"At least we have an ID for the first one," he said.

"Wish we had an ID for her killer."

Natasha Barrington and her team had the room set up. The body of the young woman was laid out, covered by a sheet.

Natasha looked up at them. "This one also has long dark hair. She's skinny too. Are you looking at the recent two murders in conjunction with the Norbury killings?"

"That isn't official," Ruth said. "Our new chief super was on the Norbury case himself, and he's convinced they got the right man."

"He may have to think again. I had a look at the old PM reports. The victims were similar in appearance to the latest two —same hair and body shape. It would seem your killer has a type."

Ruth nodded wearily. That wasn't entirely helpful. It simply added weight to the theory that DCI Boyd and his team had got the wrong man, and that Norbury was innocent. The new boss wouldn't like that.

Natasha began examining the body. "There is evidence of blunt trauma to the back of the head. Similar wound to the last one. Her hair was chin length, and it's been cut back to the scalp on one side. We'll test the hair found inside the toy. She has the brand across her midriff, the sideways-on 'T' shape. There are nail marks in her hands and feet. Similar puncture marks on the arms and legs to the first victim are present."

Ruth cast a quick glance Rocco's way. He was pale, frowning, obviously finding this as hard as she was.

"This time, the mouth was left intact."

They watched while Natasha took a look at the teeth.

"I think your victim bit her killer. There's no sign that she bit her own mouth. Give me a swab," she asked the assistant. "There is evidence of blood, even what looks like a tiny piece of flesh between her two front teeth. She must have bitten him hard. Shame it did her no good."

"Does that mean we'll get the killer's DNA this time?" Ruth asked.

"If it was him she bit," Natasha said. "You ought to consider that he left evidence behind because he was rushed, even that he was disturbed."

"I bet that empty unit is a place the homeless hang out in at night," Rocco said.

She nodded. "We'll get uniform to keep an eye on it, and ask questions. You never know."

"She died from catastrophic blood loss," Natasha said. "Like the last one, he slit her throat, cutting through the carotid artery."

"Age?" Ruth asked.

"Mid-thirties."

"Sexual interference?"

"No sign."

The two detectives watched while Natasha cut vertically into the body and started to examine the internal organs. She gasped. "She was pregnant. From the size of the foetus, I'd say about four months."

This upset Ruth. Murder of an adult was bad enough, without killing the innocent and unborn too. "We have to find out who she was, fast. Her family need to know about this. Any rings?"

"No. Not even a mark where one might have been."

Chapter 22

He held a newspaper in front of the other man's face and shook it. "Look at the bloody headline! You've risked the lot with your stupid behaviour! We spoke about this. You promised me three months ago that it wouldn't happen again. You had no intention of stopping, did you? You lied. You're a bloody fool. I don't care what happens to you, but it'll affect the operation, and that does concern me. There's too much money at stake. You killed another one. You didn't even vary the method. The police aren't daft. They'll be coming after you. I've helped you in the past but I won't risk it again. It might cost me my freedom. Sooner or later, your luck will run out."

"You need to stay calm. It'll be fine, you know it will, just like last time. I know the score. I'm good at covering my tracks. And you're lying. You do care what happens to me. You care very much."

"You're risking everything."

"I don't know why you're complaining. The killings put them off the scent. The coppers are so taken up with the murders they don't have time for our little enterprise. Apart from which, I couldn't resist. You have to understand how it is with me. That girl a few months ago, she was a gift. A loner with no past. And no future."

"I don't believe what I'm hearing. Well, I don't understand how it is with you. Here I am, a pillar of the community with an impeccable reputation. I donate to every charity going. I am well liked and respected—"

"And I'm not? You're forgetting my reputation. You mustn't worry. It'll work out fine. No one is looking in my direction. I'm quite safe. This one now, she was the same — a gift I couldn't pass up."

"How many more of your dead prey am I going to have to deal with?"

"I don't know what you mean. You didn't have to deal with the last two."

"This is murder. The police are looking for you. They'll find out about your past. They'll pull out all the stops to make sure you're caught. I don't know why I'm hesitating really. I should just turn you in myself."

"I don't think so. You're forgetting the tales I could tell. Make no mistake, you and me are in this together. It may be me that sins, but you know all about it. You even watch my little videos. Enjoy them too. That makes you just as guilty as me."

"I am not! I've never killed anyone."

"You would if you had to. But you're fortunate. You've got me to do your dirty work."

"I want it to stop! No more."

"That depends on how things go. How I feel. I can't promise."

"You will stop, or I'll tell the police myself."

"Oh no you won't. You've got too much to lose. We made a small fortune last night. The killings, the drugs — they're part of the same thing. We're a partnership."

"I am not a killer."

"No, you're a fucking bore, and I'm sick of you. I'm going out."

"Where you going?"

"Never you mind. Don't worry, I won't kill anybody."

* * *

Doc Hoyle was awake, up and about again. "Get anywhere?" he asked.

"Not with the pills, but I will have a word with Eve," Calladine replied.

"The problem we've got is twofold, Tom. The pills are one thing, but there's also the waste. If it simply gets dumped somewhere, it'll cause problems."

"You working tonight?" Calladine asked.

"Don't have any choice," said the doc. "You lot are out in force all over town. It might quieten things down, but I'm not banking on it."

"Long has been given the drugs case," Calladine said. "I hope he's giving it his all. Let me know if anyone comes in tonight who might be willing to talk to us. Who they're buying the stuff from will do, for starters."

Calladine's mobile rang. It was DCI Rhona Birch calling from the station.

"Will you come in and see me? Within the next hour if it isn't inconvenient," she said.

"Yes, ma'am. Promise you won't arrest me though."

"Very droll, Inspector. We need to talk. Put things straight. See you soon."

He smiled at the doc. "They want me back. I'm going in now to speak to Birch. About bloody time too."

Calladine was quietly optimistic that he'd be back in post before the end of the day. He decided not to tell Ruth until he was sure. Greco had done his stuff and come up with the truth, and Calladine was grateful to him. He owed the dour detective one. Perhaps a pint in the Wheatsheaf later, before Greco made his way back to Oldston.

Calladine took the road out of Hopecross into Lowermill, but instead of turning directly into Leesdon centre, he decided to take a spin around the Hobfield first. The estate was small, and from the large open space in the centre, it was possible to see all the tower blocks. The place was quiet, with hardly any movement on the streets. A couple of mums with prams, and pensioners milling about by the bus stop, but that was it. This was odd, but more worrying was the absence of any sign of activity on the part of DI Long and his team. There wasn't a uniformed officer in sight.

He checked his watch. It was nearly five p.m. A quick chat with Birch, and then back to work. Things were looking up.

Chapter 23

Calladine hadn't expected to find the new chief super closeted with Birch.

He nodded at him. "Sir. It's been a while."

"Sit down, Calladine," Ford replied.

Was this curtness good or bad? Calladine couldn't tell. Ford had always been a man of few words.

"DCI Greco has carried out a thorough investigation into the money that appeared in your bank account," Birch said. "He is satisfied that it didn't come from anyone attempting to bribe you. He came to the conclusion that you were not on the take."

Calladine smiled. "I did try to tell you."

"Do you have any idea who could be behind this generosity then?" the super asked.

"No, sir, and I've given it considerable thought. Someone wanted me out of the way, that's for sure. They kidnapped me and planted the money. Who, or why, is a complete mystery."

"This Heights Industrial," said the super. "Do you know them?"

Calladine shook his head. "The name means nothing. I've been doing some research of my own, and the company is newly established. That's as far as I've got. I need the facilities here at the station in order to take it further."

"Greco thinks you're still in danger, your sergeant's child too. What's your view?" Ford said.

"They are ruthless people. I would put nothing past them. It's a shame the Scottish police were not quicker off the mark in getting to that house."

"We're still waiting on forensics. There will be fingerprints, traces of DNA."

"It's our belief," Ford said, "that what happened to you is connected to a current investigation."

"I can't think what. I didn't even have one ongoing when I was taken. I was preparing for the Costello trial. The murders that DS Bayliss is looking into happened subsequently. As did the sudden swamping of the local area with new designer drugs."

"Nonetheless, I suggest you keep an open mind."

Ford hadn't taken him to task about any part of what had happened. Calladine wouldn't have been surprised if he had. But Ford was being reasonable.

"What happens now, sir? Do I return to work?"

"I don't see why not. Greco is keen to get back to his own station."

"We'll see you in the morning," Birch said. "DS Bayliss will be pleased. She's done well in your absence, but this murder case is a challenging one."

He was back, and about bloody time too! Calladine stood up. "Right then. Tomorrow it is."

But he didn't go home. Calladine went into the incident room. He had a lot to catch up on. Birch was right. Ruth had done a good job. The board was filled with images and information. Calladine looked around. Where were they all?

"Have they seen sense?" Greco said, coming out of Calladine's office.

Calladine nodded.

"I'm pleased. It means I can get off home."

The two men regarded each other. Calladine had got him wrong. Yes, Greco was a stickler for detail and getting at the truth. There was nothing wrong with that.

"Thanks for what you did," he said.

"The outcome is only right and proper. You didn't take a bribe, so there's no reason to keep you away from the job."

"Nonetheless, I'm grateful. If I can ever do anything for you, let me know. Speaking of which, do you fancy a pint?"

"I can't. My daughter's at home. Matilda and her aunt are expecting me."

The two shook hands and Greco walked away. His step was almost jaunty.

Calladine had his office back — and access to the police computer systems. He pushed open the door and stood for a moment on the threshold. There was not a piece of paper or file out of place. The surfaces were pristine, and even the windows had been cleaned. Tentatively, Calladine opened one of the drawers of his filing cabinet. Everything was tidy, all filed in the proper order. He'd never find anything again!

What he wanted to find was the team, to tell them he was back. He rang Ruth on her mobile.

"Where are you all? I'm in the clear. Greco did good. I felt like a pint across the road, but there's no one about."

"Rocco and I've just been at another PM at the Duggan. Rocco has gone off home. Alice will still be rummaging around in the archive if you want to speak to her."

Calladine thought about this for a moment. "No. In that case, I'll get off myself. See you all in the morning, bright and early."

Neither Birch nor Ford had said anything about the protection Greco had mentioned. Well, if someone was keeping an eye on him, Calladine hadn't noticed. He doubted they were that good. He hoped that wasn't the case with Harry.

It was dark as he walked across the car park. He could see the Wheatsheaf pub ablaze with light, and for a moment he was tempted. But he should see Layla, and tell her what had happened to him.

But Layla's car was not outside her house. Disappointed, he called her mobile. He really fancied a catch-up, something to eat and a beer.

"It's good to hear your voice. I've been worried. All that blood on your car had me jittery. But I'm on duty, love," she said. "It's cracking off all over town. It's even worse than last night. We've got kids OD'ing on these bloody blue pills. Most are off their heads and violent with it. We're parked up by the canal. One poor bloke has taken so much he can barely breathe. It's going to be a long one. So it'll have to be tomorrow, I'm afraid."

Calladine heard shouting in the background and Layla rang off. He hoped that uniform was out in force. He looked up at the dark windows of his house. He hadn't been home for days. He could hear Sam barking in Layla's house across the road. She had obviously taken him in for the duration. What to do? With another glance at his home, Calladine got back in his car. He'd take a look for himself at the mayhem erupting all over Leesdon.

* * *

Alenka dug her heels in. "Enough is enough! I've been tramping round this estate for most of the day. Lara needs some food and her bed." It was all very well for Newt to lay down the rules, but it was dark and getting wild out there. "Folk know what I've got. They're rough. They've started searching through the pram, through

Lara's things. It's not a good idea, me working for you like this."

"That's where you're wrong, babe. It's a perfect idea. Now, hand over the cash."

Alenka took a cloth pouch from her bag and handed it over. "I need money for the rent."

"No can do. This little lot has got to go to my boss."

"I've been working hard. Long hours. I deserve something," she said.

"You'll get yours when you've earned it."

"The police spoke to me."

Newt's expression hardened. "No mention of me, I hope."

"Not yet, but they'll be speaking to me again, about Ingrid. She was murdered. They've found her body."

Newt backed away, raising his hands. "Nowt to do with me." He took a couple of tenners from the bag. "Here. Now bugger off till I tell you to come back."

Chapter 24

In contrast to the afternoon, the Hobfield and the streets around the estate were abuzz with movement. The younger kids seemed to have gone wild. Groups of them, many on pushbikes, were all over the road, doing wheelies on the footpaths and in the square. Calladine had witnessed this place in many different moods, but tonight was like nothing he could remember. It was a riot. Something must have happened. The only thing he could think of was the drugs.

He parked his car outside Heron House and watched for a while. One or two older teens were moving about in the shadows. A group of them, tall and hooded, were standing in the main doorway to the tower block. He saw one of them signal to a lad on a bike. A package changed hands, and the boy rode off.

Aware that uniform must be out in force, Calladine rang the station and told the desk sergeant to pass the information on, as well as where he was parked. These lads were far too young to be dealing. Someone was running them, and they had to be stopped. Theoretically, they should be able to round up a good few of them tonight.

Get the parents involved, go from there. Problem was, they were fast.

A uniformed officer knocked on the car window. "There's a bunch of them by the garages. Me and Gary over there are going to go round the back. Would you wait at the front, sir?"

Calladine got out of his car and walked towards the low shed-like buildings. He could just make out movement. Someone was standing in the narrow gap between two of the garages. As the bikes came along, he was passing out small packages to them.

The uniforms were in place. Calladine moved forward. "What have you got there, son?"

The boy's eyes glittered at him from the dark. "You know the deal. You get nowt till I see the cash."

The uniform nodded at Calladine, who said, "Come out of there, son. You're nicked."

The lad turned slightly, no doubt hoping to make a run for it. But he was no match for the two burly uniformed policemen.

"Take him down to the station," Calladine said. "See if you can get a parent's name. I'll be along shortly."

He looked across the square. Someone had lit a fire on the waste ground between the Hobfield and the main road. The estate was no place to linger.

* * *

The lad sat, looking sullen, in the soft interview room. He was young, no more than twelve. A uniformed female PC was keeping an eye on him.

Calladine went in.

"His mother's on her way, sir," the PC said.

"Do we have a name?"

"Dane Hamilton, but that's all he's saying."

Calladine knew the surname. If the lad was from the family he was thinking of, then his father was currently doing time for robbery.

"Did his mother say how long?" he asked.

"She was in one of the pubs in Leesdon, so could be any time, sir."

Just what Calladine needed, a drunk parent! He wondered who was supposed to be taking care of the lad.

"Want a drink?" Calladine offered. "Hot or cold? We might manage a biscuit too."

The boy looked up, his expression wary. "Can't buy me with a bloody biscuit, copper. I'm no soft touch, yer know."

Calladine smiled. "Never thought you were. Just a friendly offer. Take it or leave it."

"Okay, I'll have a coke, and make sure the biscuit's a chocolate one." He grinned. "Might as well get what I can out of you lot while I'm 'ere."

It was half an hour before his mother made an appearance. It wasn't late, just after nine, but she was already the worse for drink.

"I get one night out! And what does the little bastard do? Gets picked up by the bloody coppers. Shit."

"We want to ask Dane a few questions," Calladine said.

"Make it snappy. All I want now's to get the stupid sod home."

"We suspect he was drug running on the Hobfield tonight. Dane, and a number of other youngsters. What I want to know is, who for?"

The woman's face was thunderous. "Dane! You little . . ." She started forward and extended a fist, ready to lamp him one.

Calladine stepped in front of the boy. "Whoa! Hang on there. That won't do any good."

She staggered back. "Just like his father, that one. Rotten to the core."

Young, no more than thirty, Dane's mother had dyed blonde straw-like hair. She was thin, and her skin-tight clothing, black leggings and leopard-print top made her look even thinner. Her speech was slurred.

"Would you ask Dane to turn out his pockets, please?" Calladine said.

"Why? What d'yer think he's got in there?"

"Drugs, Mrs Hamilton. And I can tell you, before the night is out we'll have a whole bunch of overdoses clogging up A&E at Leesdon General. Knowing what we're dealing with could save someone's life."

"It's Ms," she said, nose in the air. Then, before Calladine could stop her, she stepped forward and delivered a hard slap to the side of Dane's face. "That's for getting me dragged down 'ere, selfish bugger. Now, do as the policeman wants. Turn yer pockets out."

The lad rubbed his face with one hand and rummaged in the pockets of his leather jacket with the other. "Nowt much. Just a few of these."

He put several small clear bags, each containing two or three blue pills, on the table in front of them.

"Where did you get them?" Calladine said.

"Found 'em."

"Don't test my patience, lad. I know what goes on. Your job tonight was ride around the Hobfield and deliver these. Who for?"

Dane gave a sidelong look at his mother. "I tell you, I'm dead."

"Not true. No one'll know. I won't mention your name. You're quite safe."

Calladine didn't have time to intervene. Dane's mother grabbed hold of the lad's arm and gave him a shake before cuffing his ear. "Tell 'im! Tell him now, and let's get off home."

"It were Flake."

"Flake?" Calladine said. "What sort of name is that? What's his real name?"

The boy shrugged. "No idea. He's just Flake. Him and them others were handing the stuff out. Said we was to spread 'em far and wide."

"What others?"

Dane shook his head vigorously. "No idea who they are."

Calladine doubted he was telling the truth. "What about Flake?"

"Don't know his real name. He's a mate of Newt's."

"Danny Newton?" Calladine asked. That *was* a name he knew. Danny was young, about twenty, born and raised on the Hobfield.

The lad nodded.

Calladine held up one of the packets. "Do you know what these are?"

"Like I said, nowt much. Just speed."

"They're very well made. Who is Newt's supplier?"

The boy shrugged. "I don't know, but he reckons he can have all he wants. Cheap too."

Calladine realised that if the boy was telling the truth, they had a huge problem. This stuff was flooding the area.

"Can I take 'im home now?"

Calladine nodded. "We'll speak again, Dane. And I suggest you keep this little chat to yourself."

"Flake'll want the money or the stuff back. If I don't cough up, he'll beat me to a pulp."

His mother shook her head. "You're not leaving the house, lad. And you, copper, had better get this sorted. You heard 'im. He's in danger. It's down to you to keep 'im safe."

"I could give a few back," Dane chanced. "Say I couldn't get rid."

There was no way Calladine was going to let that happen. "These stay with us."

"Go on. Just a few should do it. A handful of Buckley blues to give back, and I'll be sorted."

147

Calladine looked at the boy in surprise. The two words rang in his head. *Buckley blues*. Why that name?

"What did you call the pills?"

"Buckley blues. It's what Newt said they was."

"Why did he say that?"

"Dunno. Flake reckons Newt's in with them at the factory up in the hills."

Chapter 25

"It's a tough decision to make," Ruth said. "If we go, it means I give up the only career I've ever known."

It *was* a big deal for Ruth, but Jake was shaking his head. He obviously didn't see the move as the huge wrench she did.

"You can be a detective anywhere, Ruth," he said. "Record you've got, the force in Sussex will snap you up. We go down there, I bet you make inspector in no time."

Ruth inhaled and moved the bedroom curtain to take a peek outside. There was the reassuring presence of two officers sat in a car. "That might be the case, but it isn't what I want. I like working in Leesworth. We are a team and that hasn't happened overnight. My relationship with my colleagues has grown over the years, with Calladine particularly."

"You don't have to rush into things. Even if the Sussex force don't want you, I'll be earning enough to look after all of us. You might enjoy some time with Harry. Be a young mum for a change, instead of this frantic woman who never has a minute."

So that was it. Underneath all that talk of picking up her career in a new area was the hope that she'd opt for being a stay-at-home mum. "Now you're being unfair," she said. "I spend plenty of time with Harry. He goes short of nothing."

"True, but he's very young and we'll never get this time back."

"Jake, if you're so concerned about Harry, *you* stay at home with him. And, frankly, even if the Sussex force didn't take me, I'd stack shelves in the local supermarket before I'd stay at home all day."

"Now you're being stupid."

"And you're being unfair. You want me to give up everything. What are you prepared to sacrifice? If this was me with the job offer from a different area, what would your reaction be?"

Ruth saw the look. He had never even considered it.

"Now you're twisting things," he said.

"I don't want to leave here, Jake," Ruth said firmly. "I've thought about it, but I'm afraid it just wouldn't work for me. This is where I work, this is where I live. I see no reason to change anything."

"Not even for the sake of our relationship?"

* * *

It was getting late. By the time Calladine had finished with Dane Hamilton and his mother, it was almost ten p.m. From the reports coming in, the Hobfield was still bouncing. Uniform was bringing in a constant stream of kids, and then searching the town for their parents. As anticipated, Leesdon hospital was rapidly filling up with the causalities. All of it was important and needing sorting there and then. Calladine had a couple of names, at least — Flake and Danny Newton. But overriding everything was the need to find where the pills had come from. 'Buckley blues,' Dane had called them. This had to be a reference to Buckley Pharmaceuticals, the company Eve Buckley owned. Eve Buckley: Calladine's birth mother.

He couldn't leave it. He would have to speak to her. He picked up the office phone and dialled her landline. The housekeeper answered and told him that Eve had gone to a reception in Huddersfield and would be back late. Whether he liked it or not, their talk would have to wait until morning. Manchester this afternoon, now Huddersfield. Was Eve avoiding him?

Buckley blues. Calladine couldn't get those two words out of his head. He couldn't for the life of him think what Eve's firm was doing mixed up in all this. He went through to the incident room and stared at the board. The drugs problem was one thing, but the team also had two murders to sort. The PM results were ghastly. These crimes were more than just echoes of the case he'd worked on with Boyd and the rest of them. They were dead ringers. Was it the same killer? Couldn't be. Norbury was locked away. It had to be down to someone who knew the details, and knew them intimately.

His head was pounding. It was time to go home. The drugs case was Long's anyway. He scribbled a quick note and left it on Long's desk, omitting the Buckley connection. He wanted to speak to Eve before he divulged that one. Calladine had had enough for one day.

He was on his way out of the building when the desk sergeant called him back.

"Sir, there's been an incident."

"Not the bloody Hobfield again?"

"No, sir. DI Long's been the victim of a hit and run. He's in Leesdon General, in a bad way."

* * *

So much for going home. There was no way Calladine could do that until he knew Long's condition.

When Calladine arrived at the hospital reception, Layla was there. "We were first on the scene. It was me and my partner who brought him in. According to the witness, the car was parked up. When they saw DI Long, they drove straight at him, no hesitation."

"Where was this?"

"Oldston Road."

Calladine knew that was where Long lived. Someone had been waiting for him. But why? "Do we know this witness's name?"

"John Denton. He stayed with Long until we arrived. He had the foresight to jot down the car registration number." Layla handed him a piece of paper.

"Thanks, love. What have they done with him?"

"He's in resus. They'll assess his injuries, then more than likely take him up to theatre. He was bleeding pretty badly from a head wound, and I'd say his leg was broken."

Calladine gave her a quick peck on the cheek and made his way along the corridor to the resus department.

Chapter 26

Day 6

Calladine spent most of the night with Brad Long. The DI was badly injured. As Layla had thought, he had a broken leg and the scalp wound wouldn't stop bleeding. After a CT scan, the medics decided that, despite the way his head looked, no really serious damage had been done.

The following morning, Calladine related the sorry tale to the team.

"Long's current case was the drugs. I suspect that what happened to him is directly related. It's an extremely lucrative business someone's got going. Word must have got round that he was the detective in charge, and a decision made to take him out. That means whoever we are dealing with is one ruthless bastard. Any ideas?"

"There are no rumours circulating," Rocco said. "In fact, I'd say there's a power vacuum right now. No one has taken over since Costello."

"Perhaps someone from out of town?" Ruth suggested. "Seen the area going begging and stepped in big time. How's DI Long doing?"

"He's having surgery on his leg this morning. I'll visit him later and ask him what he remembers. See what you can find out. We need to discover who is producing the pills, and quick."

"Do we know *where* they are being produced, sir?" Alice asked.

What should he say? "I'm working on that one. I'll be able to give you more information later."

Ruth reminded him about the murders. "We have two bodies in the morgue, don't forget. We have an ID for the first one but not the second. That needs putting right."

"Missing persons?"

"Nothing yesterday," Rocco said. "And there was nothing on her that might help."

"She was about four months pregnant," Ruth said. "I'll follow up on that today. If she made herself known to the ante-natal clinic, they might be able to help us."

Calladine nodded at her. "Good call. Take Alice with you."

"What about the Norbury angle?" Rocco asked.

"What about him?" Calladine asked.

Rocco frowned. "Are we sure it was Norbury in the first place?"

"We had evidence, a confession. The CPS were satisfied, and we had no one else in the frame at the time," Calladine said, but in truth that case still bothered him.

"You did voice doubts," Ruth said.

"I don't know. There was just something about him. He'd chop and change his story so much it was hard to keep tabs. But then all that stopped. It was as if he'd been practising his confession and finally got the whole thing straight. In the end, he was word perfect."

"You think he was coached?" Ruth said. "Or bullied perhaps? I read in the log that after one interview, he turned up for the following one with a bruise on his face. Is that a possibility?"

"I wasn't here for most of the investigation. I don't know who I'd pin that on if it was true. Norbury's a strange character. If you read the transcripts, he said all sorts of things."

"If not Norbury, then who?" Ruth said.

"We need to check who might know the details. The investigating team, maybe? Other prisoners Norbury could have told? I'll have to speak to Birch. We don't want to upset anyone."

"By anyone, you mean Angus Ford, I presume. He does appear to be a tad sensitive about the issue." Ruth grimaced.

Calladine smiled at her. "He's sensitive about everything to do with his job. Mind you, it was a big case and he was a member of the team that cracked it. He was made up to DI not long after. The Norbury case was just one in a string of cases that he was party to solving that year. His career never looked back. He certainly wouldn't want anything or anyone casting doubt on the Norbury or any other conviction he was involved in. Not that he had a big part to play. He was like me, off on a course for most of it."

"I'll check out what became of the investigating team," Rocco said, "particularly Boyd and Andrews, and as many of the others I can find who were involved at the time. There's SOCO too."

"Good," Calladine said. "We'll have a case conference after lunch."

Rocco was already standing up. "What are you up to, sir?"

"I have to go and have a word with someone urgently. It's connected with the investigations, but I'll say more about it later."

* * *

Calladine had to see Eve. He needed to find out what she knew about the pills. It could not be simple coincidence that Dane Hamilton had referred to them as 'Buckley blues.' This time he didn't phone first. He wanted to surprise her.

Eve Buckley lived in a huge house halfway up one of the hills that surrounded Leesdon. It was built of stone and had stood resplendent in its situation, looking down over the town, for over a hundred years. Buckley's factory, a former paper mill, was only a few hundred yards below.

Calladine rang the bell and waited on the doorstep, wondering whether Eve knew what was going on in the town. If she did, what then? He couldn't believe she was complicit in the manufacture of those blue pills.

Eve's housekeeper finally answered the door.

"Is Eve in?" he asked.

She smiled. "Come in. Mrs Buckley will be pleased to see you."

Calladine doubted that, not once he explained the reason for his visit.

The housekeeper led him into a large sitting room. Eve was sitting on a sofa, sorting through a pile of paperwork. She looked up, surprised.

"It's all very well Simon going away, but it leaves me with this little lot to deal with." She stood up and kissed his cheek. "Sorry about yesterday. I had appointments I couldn't get out of. I wasn't expecting you to visit. I was told you'd gone away for a few days. You've hurt your face." She brushed her fingertips gently over the bruise. "What happened?"

He shrugged. "It was something and nothing."

"Would you like some tea or coffee?"

"No thank you."

Eve's hair was dark, cut into an elegant bob, and the clothes she wore were casual but expensive. She looked her usual smart self. But there was something about her. It was in the body language. She seemed ill at ease, like someone waiting for questions she didn't want to answer.

After an uncomfortable silence, she cleared her throat. "I had Zoe on the phone asking about you. I had no idea what to tell her. The few days away, to re-charge your batteries was it?"

He shrugged again. "Not really."

"Work then?"

"It's work now." Calladine was growing impatient with the small talk. "Are you aware of what's going on in the area? Do you know anything about the drug dealing that's taking place?"

"Why would I know anything about that?" She looked genuinely puzzled at his question, and her tone was indignant.

Calladine scratched his head. She had to know something. Her factory and staff couldn't be part of this without her knowledge.

"I don't even read the papers," she said. "They print rubbish, the lot of them."

"Leesdon and other areas have been swamped with a drug that's being manufactured locally." He paused, waiting for a response that didn't come. "I believe that these drugs are being made in your factory, Eve."

"That can't be right! If that were true, I'd know about it. My staff would never allow anything illegal to happen."

"The evidence is building. If you know anything, or suspect anything, you have to tell me."

She turned her back to him. "It's not that easy, Tom."

"What do you mean? Has something happened?"

She faced him, her expression troubled. Was that fear he saw in her eyes? "Yes, and more will follow if I talk. They've already hurt you. They promised me you'd be safe, that you wouldn't be harmed."

Calladine stared at her. She meant his kidnap. "We'll talk about that shortly. I'm here about these." He took out his phone and showed her the photo of the blue pills. "Can you tell me anything about them?"

She lowered her voice to a whisper. "No, what are they?" She stepped through the French doors, out into the garden.

Calladine followed her. "The pills, Eve. This is important. What do you know about them? The kids on the Hobfield are calling them 'Buckley blues.' From the name, they must have something to do with your company."

"What sort of pills are they?"

"Speed."

All colour drained from Eve's face. "This is all my fault. I should have done more when it first started. Instead, I went along with what they wanted. But I was frightened. Nothing like this has ever happened to me before."

"You knew about the drugs?" Calladine could hardly believe what he was hearing. The community trusted this woman. She employed dozens of them, and now he was finding that she was overseeing the production of drugs that threatened their health, their very lives!

"Last night," he said, "a colleague of mine, the detective investigating the drug dealing, was deliberately mown down by a car and badly injured. You have to tell me what you know before someone gets killed."

The look on her face said it all. She was devastated. "I've been an old fool. But I was so scared, Tom. I was told that if I didn't do as I was told, they would harm you, Zoe too and then they'd start on the families of your team."

"Harm me? What's that supposed to mean?"

"They weren't joking. It was a very real threat. And then when you disappeared . . ." She shook her head.

Suddenly it all fell into place. "That's why I was kidnapped!"

"Yes. They took you and then blackmailed me. They wanted access to one of the factory outbuildings, the one further up the hill. Not only that, they wanted chemicals

158

delivered and invoiced to Buckley's. If I refused, they said they'd kill you. I couldn't take that risk. When you suddenly vanished, I was frantic, but they assured me that you'd be set free once they'd finished. I had no idea what they were up to. When I saw what was on the list of stuff, I should've realised. But even if I had, I dared not risk your life.

"They set things up to make it look as if I'd run out on everyone. Taken a bribe." Calladine nodded sombrely. "That got me into no end of trouble."

"I did leave you clues." She gave him a half-hearted smile. "You *are* a detective. I thought it was worth a shot."

"Clues?" Calladine frowned.

"Heights Industrial? My company was Heights Pharmaceuticals before it became Buckley's. I just used false names for the directors. This house is called 'The Heights.'"

Calladine closed his eyes for a moment. He should have realised. "The money?"

"I put that in your account. They made me. I think they wanted the police to believe that you'd taken a bribe. I have no idea why. I can only presume that they wanted you and your disappearance to keep your colleagues busy. It gave them time to get production of those pills set up without hindrance from the police."

"Surely your staff must have known what was going on?"

"No, they didn't. I told my manager, Alan Landseer that we'd let the building out. It's an old building and, as a rule, no one goes up there. Alan is too busy with his own job to stick his nose in elsewhere."

"Do you know the place they took me to?"

"Moortop Manse? Yes. It's Buckley property. Years ago, when my husband was alive, it was used for corporate events. Shooting weekends when the grouse were in season. Nowadays, it's rented out to hiking clubs, and none of the family ever go there. I said they could use it to keep you in. I was worried that the alternative would be a damp cellar somewhere."

"Who is blackmailing you?"

Eve didn't reply. Instead, she set off in the direction of a summer house at the bottom of the garden.

Calladine followed her. "You must tell me. I have to put a stop to it."

"They know you're on to them. Don't you see? That's why your colleague was targeted. The next one on their hit list will be you, Tom. I can't take that risk."

"Who, Eve? Tell me. I can put a stop to this, I promise you. And it's not just Brad Long who has suffered. They have threatened Ruth's son, Harry."

She turned and faced him. "That's truly dreadful, but I don't know." She held up her hand. "I really don't. Everything was done over the phone, or by text. I never actually met anyone face to face."

"Have they been in touch with you since I escaped?"

"No. But now I'm terrified they'll take another member of my family, Samantha or my grandson, David. Neither of them would cope. They know nothing about it."

"Can I take the mobile they contacted you on?"

"Yes. It's in the house."

"Are they still using the outbuilding?"

Eve nodded.

"We'll raid the place and arrest whoever we find there."

Chapter 27

Still reeling, Calladine returned to the station.

"We might have an identity for the second body," Ruth said. "Alice and I got nowhere at the antenatal clinic, but a bloke came in this morning and reported his partner, Kelly Donald, missing. He told the desk sergeant that she hasn't been home in a couple of days, and that's just not like her. Also, like our victim, she is four months pregnant."

"Will he have a look at her for us?"

"Yes. I'm meeting him at the Duggan at one." She looked at him. "What have you been up to?"

"Tell you later." He needed a word with Birch before he broadcast what he knew. "Have we got the data we requested from Ingrid Plesec's phone provider?"

"I'll get on to them again," Rocco said.

"Do that. Tell them it's urgent."

Birch was at her desk. She didn't look pleased. "I've had the chief super on. He wants action on what happened to you. Greco's needed by central Manchester, so he's no longer investigating. It's down to us, I'm afraid."

Calladine groaned inwardly. They had two murders, the drug problem, and now he was supposed to solve his own kidnapping!

"Won't that be a conflict of interest, ma'am?"

She heaved a sigh. "You're right. Get DS Bayliss to look into it. DS Thorpe can help too. He'll be at a loose end now that Long is in hospital."

Now for the revelation. "As it happens, I have made a breakthrough. I was kidnapped, and my continued safety used as a lever, in order to blackmail Eve Buckley."

Birch stared at him. "Your *mother*?"

Calladine nodded. "As you are aware, she owns the Buckley pharmaceutical company. The drugs that are currently swamping Leesworth are being produced in a building belonging to her factory."

"Is she complicit in this?"

"No, ma'am. As I said, Eve is being blackmailed. She is terrified. They're telling her that if she refuses to do as she's told, I come off worst. She's been living in terror for days."

"Who told you this?"

"Eve herself. I became suspicious because of something I heard one of the kids say when I was talking to him, so I went to see her."

Birch's eyes were wide. "And the money? What did she have to say about that?"

"She put the money into my account. Eve has the paper trail if you require evidence. She had no idea what it was about, but we know it was intended to fit me up as a bribe-taker."

"She volunteered this information?" Birch looked doubtful.

"She had no choice. I had evidence to suggest that the pills came from her factory. When I confronted her with it, she admitted everything."

"How do we know that Mrs Buckley isn't party to the crime?"

"She has nothing to gain from it. She certainly doesn't need the money. And I was kidnapped."

Birch was silent for a few moments. "So, what do we do next?"

"I suggest we raid that outbuilding," Calladine said. "Arrest everyone, and go from there."

"Very well. I'll mobilise uniform. DS Thorpe can go too." Birch raised her finger. "Do not warn Mrs Buckley that this is about to happen. I'll tell Thorpe. We need movement on the murder cases. Now that you're back, see to it."

Calladine went back to the incident room. "I'll come to the Duggan with you, Ruth," he said. "Speak to the partner."

Alice put down the phone receiver. "Sir? I rang the prison yesterday, and asked about George Norbury. They've just got back to me. Norbury is dead. He did have someone he was friendly with, a man called Keith Wrigley, also in for murder. They talked a lot, apparently. Wrigley was released on license six months ago. He lives in Rochdale, not far away."

"You think Wrigley has carried on where Norbury left off?"

She nodded. "It's possible."

"At the very least, we should check him out. See what he's been up to. See if you can arrange to speak to him, will you, Alice?"

"We traced Andrews," Rocco said. "He's been living in New Zealand for the last six years, so I think we can cross him off the list. Also, DCI Boyd died last year, so not him either."

"The phone data?" Calladine asked.

"Ingrid's phone provider is emailing it across this morning," Rocco said.

"I've got another one for you." Calladine handed Rocco Eve's mobile. "Have a look at the calls and texts received. We could do with knowing who sent them. If, as

I suspect, they were sent from a pay-as-you-go, try and get a location. The provider should help."

Rocco scrolled through the texts. "Most of these are pretty short, guv. They don't give much away."

"Go through them carefully, Rocco. If you do spot anything, ring me. The registration number for the car that had a go at DI Long, give it to Thorpe, will you?"

Long was his DI after all, so Thorpe could do some of the legwork. They had enough on their plates. Calladine glanced at the incident board. Still nothing much on the first killing. He turned to Ruth. "What about the forensics on Ingrid Plesec?"

"Julian has given it his all, but he can't find a thing. The killer must have covered up well and used gloves."

Calladine nodded. "Knew what he was doing."

"The second one is different. He was probably disturbed. Let's get over to the Duggan. We can have a chat to Julian before the victim's partner turns up. You can tell me what you've been up to on the way." Ruth smiled at him.

"I spent some time with Brad Long last night. He was lucky. He'll hobble about for a while, but he should make a good recovery. This morning, I went for a chat with Eve."

"Did you tell her what happened to you?" Ruth asked.

He handed her the car keys. "You drive, I'll talk."

They got into the car and Ruth drove out. "Sounds like you've a lot to say."

"A lot to think about for sure. It turns out that Eve was responsible for what happened to me." At this, Ruth almost swerved. "Part of her factory is producing the speed that's being sold all over Greater Manchester. She is, or was, being blackmailed. Refuse to do as she was told, and I got hurt. You know the drill."

"And the money?" Ruth asked.

"Eve again. It was her money."

"I appreciate you don't really know her very well, but you can't seriously think that she was involved!" Ruth glanced at him.

"No, I don't, but that's not how the CPS might see it. She will more than likely be taken to task over this. Several aspects are puzzling. Not least — why me? Eve has other, closer family members. Take her young grandson, David, for instance. If he was taken, that would really up the pressure."

"But what about his mother, your half-sister Samantha? Wouldn't she know what was going on? Perhaps they weren't prepared to take that risk."

"I hadn't thought of that," Calladine said. "But it still niggles. If I was the one in charge, my first choice wouldn't be me."

"Perhaps the reason was twofold. You are Eve's son, but they also wanted you out of the way for some other reason."

He shook his head. "Can't think what that would be."

They pulled into the Duggan carpark, and Ruth checked her watch. "Shall we have a word with Julian first?"

"Have you spoken to Jake about the job yet?" Calladine asked.

"He wants to go. I don't. To be honest with you, it's tearing us apart."

"I don't know what to suggest."

"As far as I can see, there's nothing to be done. Jake won't change his mind and neither will I. At this rate, we'll be meeting up at weekends, halfway along the M1."

"Tom, you're back!" Julian Batho was waiting for them at the end of the corridor. "Properly back, I mean, not skulking around in backstreet cafés."

Calladine smiled. "You've been talking to the doc."

"I haven't found anything of help at the second kill site," Julian said. "I think Natasha was right when she reckoned your second victim tried to fight him off at some point. I've had a look at the body, including the mouth. The fragment of flesh found in her teeth is being DNA tested. There are also some marks on her hands that could be defence wounds. I've had a word with Natasha and she agrees. I've also examined the toy bear. It was stuffed with human hair like the last one. I'll do tests to check if it is the victim's hair."

"That it, Julian?"

"It's more than we got with the first victim. Your killer is careful, but this time he didn't wear gloves. We found a single fingerprint in a smear of blood, but it's too indistinct to get a match. With regard to the first victim, there's no foreign DNA or prints. Neither have we found anything useful among the detritus left in the old church."

"Okay. As soon as the tests are complete, let me know if the DNA throws up a match. We're just about to ID the second one."

They walked back towards the morgue. The second victim's partner, a man called Geoff Blackshaw, was sitting waiting for them just outside. "I'm dreading this," he said. "It'll be my Kelly, I just know it."

"Isn't there anywhere else she could have gone?" Ruth asked.

Blackshaw shook his head. "No. As soon as she's finished her shift at the hospital, she's straight home."

The technician was ready for them. He pulled back the sheet covering the woman's face.

Chapter 28

Calladine pinned a photo to the board. "Our second victim is called Kelly Donald. Her partner has just identified her. This is her photo. She worked as a cleaner at the hospital. Leesdon General has CCTV everywhere. Rocco, get over there and take a look. The night she failed to go home, the weather was bad, and it would have been dark by the time she finished her shift. She'd have been wrapped up, so you'll have to look hard."

"Eve Buckley rang while you were out. She'd like to speak to you," Joyce said.

"It might be important. She may have remembered something else. I'll ring her from my office. Rocco, chase up the mobile records, will you?"

"Sir," Alice called out. "Keith Wrigley, that friend of Norbury's in prison, has absconded. There has been nothing on the news, but he's been out for six months and missing for the last three. I spoke to the Rochdale police. They think he could be living rough somewhere, possibly in our area. He was obsessed with Norbury apparently, saw him as some sort of hero. And now they tell me that Norbury died three months ago."

They'd never speak to him now. "Get a description and circulate it to uniform. If he is in Leesworth, we want him found, and fast."

Calladine sat at his desk, expecting that Eve wanted to speak to him because everything was kicking off at the factory. But it wasn't that at all.

"I'm hosting a party tomorrow night at the Leesworth Hall Hotel. I realise that it's probably not the best time, given what's happened, but I have no choice. It's to celebrate a contract Simon won in Japan. It's business, but I'd like you to come. Samantha will be there, and David."

"Not Simon?"

"No, he's not due back for another couple of weeks. The do is as much for the Chamber of Commerce and other local worthies as anything."

Calladine wasn't keen. The do would be formal. A quick pint in the Wheatsheaf was more his style. "Do I bring someone?"

"I thought you could ask Layla. I haven't met her properly, and it'd be the perfect opportunity."

"Okay. I'll get back to you. It depends on her shift pattern. If she can't make it, I'll bring Ruth."

"Something I should know?" Eve asked.

"Absolutely nothing. Ruth is a good friend. She'll be bailing me out if Layla can't make it. I'd do the same for her."

"Your lot have been here. They made a bit of a mess."

Here it was.

"The police have arrested six people and confiscated dozens of large boxes. I'm worried, Tom. I doubt the people who threatened me and kidnapped you will just roll over and take it."

"Is there someone with you?" he asked.

"A female officer. Also, there is a patrol car passing the house every so often. But I'm worried about Sam and David. They don't know anything about all this."

"You'll be fine. They won't dare kidnap anyone else now. They know we're on to them. Their operations at your factory are finished."

Calladine went to see Birch. "Do we know any of those arrested at Buckley's, ma'am?"

"They are all foreign with hardly any English. They were brought to Leesdon together and put to work. I doubt we'll get very much, Calladine. They only ever met one man. We have a description. It might help."

* * *

Danny Newton was lying low. Word spread fast, and he'd found out about the police raid on the factory within an hour of it happening. Miles would want to lay the blame at someone's feet and Danny was the obvious candidate.

He was holed up at his mate Flake's flat on the Hobfield. Andy Prior had acquired the nickname because of his reluctance to take part in anything involving Newt. 'Flakey matey,' Newt called him. But Newt was a bully, and usually managed to convince Flake that he needed in.

"What the hell happened?" Newt said. "You were supposed to keep an eye on the factory."

Flake shrugged. "It's in the middle of bloody nowhere. They should have been safe enough."

"Well, they weren't, were they? And now they're banged up, the lot of them. The boss'll have my balls for this." Newt didn't use Miles's name. He was the only person on the estate who knew the businessman was involved. He also knew that if he valued his life, it had to stay that way. "Any news on the car? Have they found it yet?"

"How should I know? What did you do with it anyway?" Flake asked.

"I dumped it and torched it. Just by the res on the layby near the path that goes around Bin Green. I did a good job too. Now it's your turn to be useful. Get out there. Speak to the lads. Find out what's happening. Any sign of the boss's car, leg it."

"Do we have any pills stockpiled?" Flake asked.

Newt shrugged. "A few boxes. Not enough to raise the money I'll need if the boss decides to come after me and I have to do one."

"How did the police find out about the factory?" Flake asked.

"No idea. Trashing that copper wasn't my idea. It was supposed to keep them busy, give them something else to think about. Didn't work, did it? Bet the boss'll think that's down to me too." Newt sighed.

* * *

Flake went out into the square. A group of younger kids stood around, arguing loudly. As he passed them, one called out.

"Oi, Flake! Where's your mate? Bet he's paid you alright, hasn't he? It's not fair, leaving us till last."

This irritated Flake. He didn't like everyone thinking he worked for Newt. He marched across to them. "You shouldn't hang about here, you'll attract the wrong sort of attention. There's coppers everywhere. Go on, do one!"

"We want our money. We did alright last night. Handed over hundreds to Newt. He was supposed to cough up this morning," the youth said.

Flake eyed the lad suspiciously. "Dane, isn't it?"

The lad nodded.

"There ain't no money, and there won't be for a while. Newt's in hiding. The coppers are looking for him. Me too."

"He promised me fifty. This isn't fair! We did our bit. We shifted loads of gear."

The last thing Flake wanted was this lot on his back. Newt should be the one getting all the bellyache, but he wasn't about to show his face. The kids were looking at each other, muttering and swearing. "Look, I'm sorry, right? But it is how it is." Flake turned and began to walk away.

"Newt's taking the piss. He's gotta have some respect!" Dane Hamilton yelled after him. "Stop! Talk to us. Don't treat us like fucking kids!"

Flake took no notice. The kid was a hothead. He walked away, hands in his jeans pockets. He was fed up. For years he'd been hanging onto Newt's coat tails and look where it had got him. Nowhere. The bloke was a loser. Suddenly he heard a deafening bang. Somebody screamed. Flake spun round. Dane Hamilton was brandishing a gun at him. He'd fired one shot into the sky and scared everyone to death.

"Where is he? Tell me, Flake, or I'll blast your fucking head off!"

The lad was small, not yet in his teens. What the hell was going on?

Chapter 29

Within minutes of the gunshot, police cars filled the square outside Heron House. Dane Hamilton and his mates were gathered up and taken away. Flake was shaking. He'd seen guns before, but this was the first time he'd had one waved at him. He was taken, in a separate car, to Leesdon police station.

Calladine remembered Dane. He remembered his mother too. He instructed uniform to find her and bring her in. Meanwhile, he decided to speak to Flake. Dane had told him it was Flake that had given him the pills.

Calladine smiled at him. "What's your real name?"

"Andy Prior," Flake said.

"So why do they call you Flake?"

The young man shrugged. "It's what people call me. Don't know why."

"You've been giving pills to the younger element on the estate. Then you've been getting them to do your dirty work for you and distribute them. The products from your little enterprise are currently being sold all over Greater Manchester."

"You can't pin this on me. I ain't done nothing. I've never had anything to do with pills, or drugs."

"Who do we pin it on then, Flake? Care to give us some names?"

Flake shook his head, sullen.

"We'll search your home. Your clothing. We can do tests and find out if you've handled drugs recently." Calladine waited.

Flake looked rattled. "It was just a bit of speed, for our own use, like."

"It was hardly that. You took over an entire factory. You were producing your little blue pills on an industrial scale."

Calladine looked at the young man sitting in front of him. He was shabbily dressed, in scruffy jeans, a worn T-shirt and a jacket that wasn't suitable for the weather. Someone was making a great deal of money from this, but it wasn't him. "Who are you working for? Danny Newton?"

"No one. Just me and a mate. We had this idea and—"

"Which mate? What's his name?"

Flake shrugged. "Can't remember."

"Who is it you're frightened of? There has to be someone big behind this. You didn't organise it all on your own."

"Organise what? Like I said, it's just a bit of speed."

Calladine shook his head resignedly. "Okay. Tell me how you got the factory owner onside."

"What do you mean?"

"Well, you can't just walk in, take over a building belonging to a pharmaceutical company, order stock, start your own production and expect no one to notice."

Flake looked down. "We just turned up and got on with it."

"Rubbish! Who's behind this? Who are you protecting?"

Before he could answer, Rocco walked in.

"I want Danny Newton finding and bringing in," Calladine said. "Try the Hobfield. Ask around."

"You won't find him," Flake said.

Calladine didn't like the smirk on his face. "Lock this one up until he decides to be a little more helpful."

* * *

Mandy Hamilton arrived while Calladine was interviewing Flake. He found her sitting with her son Dane in the soft interview room.

She scowled at him. "Second time this bloody week. Little bastard must think I've nothing better to do."

"I'm afraid this time it's a bit more serious, Ms Hamilton. Dane was caught with a gun. He fired off one shot, and then threatened to shoot another young man."

Her face was a picture. Her mouth dropped open and she turned to her son, hardly able to get the words out. "Who gave you a bloody gun?"

Dane looked away, silent. He kept picking at the sleeves of his jumper, which was beginning to unravel.

"Who gave you the damn thing!" she screamed. "Tell me, Dane, or I'll let them lock you away for a long, long time!"

"Newt gave it me," he whispered. "I didn't mean to fire it. I got angry and it went off by mistake."

"Do you know where Newt got it from?" Calladine asked.

"Some Mr Big he keeps on about."

"Does this Mr Big have a proper name?"

"I guess," Dane said. "But we don't know it. Newt won't say. Bloke could be anyone."

Calladine had a bad feeling. If Dane was right, if there was a new villain out there, one who wanted his identity kept secret, they were in trouble.

"Are you sure you don't have a name for this Mr Big?" He gave the lad a few moments to think about it.

"You see, Dane, you're in a lot of trouble. And I can't do much about it this time. But if you help us catch the real culprits, things could go easier for you when this comes to court."

At the word 'court,' Mandy Hamilton gasped.

"I don't know nowt," Dane said. "Even if I did, I wouldn't grass. I'd get shot myself."

"Back to the guns." Calladine remembered that Henry Johns, who'd been holed up in the old church with the child, had also had a gun. "Been dishing them out, has Newt? Who else has got one?"

Dane shrugged. "How am I s'posed to know? But he can get as many as he needs. It's a dirty business he's mixed up in."

Wasn't it just! Calladine shook his head. "What else do you know about the drugs, Dane?"

"Nowt. I just deliver 'em. I ride around the estate on my bike, drop off the pills and collect the payment. I take the money back to Flake or Newt, job done."

Mandy Hamilton stared at her son, her mouth open. "You're twelve years old, for Chrissake! Where the hell has this come from?"

"I have to do summat to earn a crust," Dane whined. "I need stuff."

"Being in possession and using a firearm is a serious offence, Ms Hamilton. We can't just let Dane go."

"Dane, son, if you know something, anything at all, you have to tell the inspector. I don't want you locked up like your dad. You won't like it. It'll stay with you for life."

Wise words, but the lad didn't look interested.

His mother turned to Calladine. "What will happen to him? What am I going to tell his dad?"

"That loser." The lad snorted.

"Dane is a minor, a child. He'll be taken to a secure unit where he'll be looked after till his trial," Calladine said.

"Can't I take him home? Give him a good hiding?"

Calladine shook his head. "I'm afraid not."

Mandy Hamilton was crying in earnest now. She'd obviously had no idea what her son had been up to.

"We'll have to search your home," Calladine said.

"Why? What do you expect to find?"

"More weapons? Drugs? Until we do a search, we don't know."

She sighed. "Do what you want. I've had it with the little bastard. His father's a rogue, but even he's never been this bad. He's doing time for thieving, nowt like what this one's got himself into."

Chapter 30

"I want you to go. You're upsetting Lara," Alenka Plesec said. She stood with the child in her arms, watching Newt, who was peering through the net curtains at the square below. She could tell he was worried, nervous about all the activity outside.

"Bloody coppers are all over the place," he muttered. "I want you to get out there, find out what's going on. Who they've arrested."

"No. It's raining. I'm not taking Lara out in this."

"Leave the kid here, then. I'll watch her."

No way that Alenka was going to do that.

Newt had come crashing into her flat about an hour ago, all riled up. From his garbled account, she gathered that one of the kids had tried to shoot Flake. "That kid the coppers took, he'll talk. He'll want to save his own skin," he said.

"And why shouldn't he? He's only a child. You shouldn't have used him."

"You know shit. Just do as you're told. I want to know what's going on, what the coppers know. Cross me, Alenka, and you'll suffer."

Alenka took several steps back. Perhaps it was better to go outside, rather than stay in the flat with him. In this mood, Newt was volatile, dangerous. She was afraid for her safety, and Lara's.

"Okay. I'll get Lara ready."

"No. On second thoughts, leave her here." He gave her a sly smile. "Then if you cross me, you have only yourself to blame for the consequences."

"I can't do that. She'll cry. She's not happy when we're apart."

"Stick her in her cot and do as you're told."

"No. I will not leave her."

"You will, or you'll get some of this."

Alenka gasped. He'd produced a gun from somewhere. This was a nightmare. She felt sick. He waved the weapon at her and she saw he meant it. She'd have to do what he wanted. She had no choice. Alenka still had Ruth's card in her coat. She decided that as soon as she was out of the flat, she'd phone the detective and ask for help.

* * *

"Sir, have you got a minute?" Rocco asked Calladine.

But just at that moment the office phone rang. It was Alenka, asking for Ruth. Calladine took the call and handed the phone to her.

"What have you got, Rocco?" Calladine asked.

"Something a little odd," Rocco said. He'd been poring over the mobile phone data.

But Ruth interrupted. "I think we may have a situation. That was Alenka Plesec. Her sister was the first victim. She says Danny Newton is holed up in her flat on the Hobfield, and her child is in there with him. He has a gun and he's threatened them both."

"Let's get going. Organise armed response," Calladine called to Alice. "Tell them to meet us outside . . . ?"

"Heron House," Ruth said. "Alenka lives at number four on the first floor."

Calladine nodded. "You and me, then."

They ran out of the building and got into the car.

"These guns, where are they getting them from?" Ruth asked.

"God knows, but it has to be stopped. Where's Alenka?" Calladine asked.

"She's hiding in the entrance to the tower block. Newt sent her outside to find out what was going on. He's obviously rattled."

"He'll be anxious that the lads might talk. Danc Hamilton hasn't said much yet, but he will. Flake too. He won't want to go down for longer than he needs."

They pulled up outside Heron House. The place was eerily quiet. Armed response hadn't arrived yet, but there were no youngsters to be seen anywhere. Alenka Plesec was standing in the doorway of the block of flats, shaking, tears streaming down her face.

"Please! You have to get Lara out of there. If she cries too much, he'll hurt her. He's not a nice man. He has a bad temper."

"Did you see the gun?" Calladine asked her.

She nodded, sobbing.

"You stay with her," Calladine said to Ruth. "I'm going up."

"Be careful, Tom!" she called after him.

Too bloody true he would. He'd had enough rough stuff this week to last him a while. He walked along the first floor deck. The curtains of the flat were closed. He tried the door. It was locked.

"Newt!" he called. "Come out. It's over."

"Do one, copper, or the kid'll come off worst."

"Don't be stupid," Calladine said. "You'll only make things worse for yourself. Don't add anything more serious to the list of charges against you. Besides, there's nowhere for you to go, and no one to help you. Your friends'll talk. It'll go better for you if you come quietly."

Calladine stood and listened. He could hear the child crying inside the flat. Danny Newton was shouting at her, swearing. He was losing it. "Come on, Newt, you're not doing anyone any good with this. You can't win."

Suddenly the door swung open. Newt had the gun in his hand, pointed at Calladine's head. "Right. You and me're going for a little walk."

"The child?" Calladine asked.

"She's alright. She's in her cot."

Calladine walked in front of him, slowly, the gun jammed into his back. This young man was seething with anger. For all Calladine knew, he could be high on some of the stuff he'd been peddling.

"Where are we going?"

Newt grunted, "Round the back."

Calladine took a quick glimpse down at the square. He could see Ruth and Alenka below. Ruth waved at him. Armed response had arrived, and were getting set up. "Can I speak to my colleagues? Let them know the child is okay?"

"Shut it and move," screamed Newt.

"There are marksmen down there, Newt. They've got their guns trained on your head. You need to stop this now. You carry on and they'll shoot you."

Calladine heard him groan behind him. The gun no longer pressed at his back. He looked over his shoulder. Newt had grabbed hold of the deck railing and was looking down. "Do something! Tell them to go away!"

"They won't do that. You have to come with us, Newt. It's all over."

"No! You'll lock me up and that's not fair."

"Put the gun down, come with me, and we'll talk about it. You can tell me your side of it."

Newt looked at him. He seemed puzzled. "Hey. You're supposed to be dead. Dead, and buried on some Scottish hillside."

"We'll talk about that too."

"Wasn't my idea. That was down to the big boss."

"And that is?"

Newt shook his head. "You don't get me that easy, copper. I say anything about him and I really am dead. In custody, locked away, it won't make no difference. He can get at me anywhere." Newt leaned forward and put his face close to Calladine's. "He has contacts in high places, see."

Chapter 31

Keith Wrigley hated living rough. As far as he could see, the only positive was that no one recognised him anymore. He'd seen his face on the front page of the local papers. That meant the police were looking. But he'd grown a beard and his hair was longer. He was now a far cry from the clean shaven, short-haired jailbird of a few months ago.

He'd been released on license, and for a little while had stayed, as agreed, with his brother in Heywood, just outside Rochdale. He enjoyed his freedom — simple things like the garden, and being able to go down to the betting shop of an afternoon.

But all that changed when he heard the news that George Norbury had died in prison.

George's death brought it all back, along with the promise he'd made to his friend. They'd talked a lot, and over time had come to trust each other. They'd shared confidences. Wrigley had killed a man, and knew perfectly well that he was guilty as convicted. But he'd done his time, and was no longer considered a danger. Norbury, on the other hand, always insisted on his innocence. He'd killed no one. He'd been set up, he said, told to take what was coming to him and keep silent. In or out of prison, it made no difference. His life depended on it.

When Wrigley first heard his story, it had sounded just like so many others. Prisoners were always telling anyone who would listen that they were innocent. Everyone was the victim of a miscarriage of justice. But there was something about George's tale, and the man himself, that had convinced Wrigley. Over the years, George had grown tired of his situation. Initially, the man who'd set him up had threatened to kill his sister if he talked. But Iris was dead now, so there was nothing to lose by coming clean.

George had made Wrigley promise to go to the police and tell them, and explicitly to see CID at Leesdon. Apparently, one of the team that had nicked him still worked there.

Wrigley had left his brother's home in Heywood without saying a word to anyone, and travelled the few miles on foot. He'd sometimes stayed the night in homeless hostels, but mostly he'd slept rough. They might be looking for him, but he was invisible. Within a short time, he'd become one of the many haunting the streets of Greater Manchester. He needed this time to work out what he would say. George had only told him so much. He said he hadn't killed anyone. He said he'd been set up, but he never told Wrigley who by. Wrigley was well aware that without a name, the police were unlikely to take any of what he had to say seriously. Nevertheless, he was determined to give it a go.

Now Wrigley stood facing the desk sergeant at Leesdon nick. He saw the distaste on the man's face when he looked at him. "I have to speak to someone. It's important. It's about an old case, and you lot need to know the truth."

"See that little room over there?" The sergeant pointed. "Sit in there. I'll get you a cup of tea. Anyone in particular you want to see?"

"Someone who worked on the Norbury case."

* * *

Calladine and Rocco sat facing Danny Newton, with the duty solicitor next to him. Newt didn't look at all bothered by what was happening. He kept checking the interview room clock.

"Need to be somewhere, Danny?" Calladine asked. "That's a shame, because you're not going anywhere for a long time. Of course, if you talk to us, things might go easier for you."

"Nowt to say, copper."

Calladine smiled. "You see, that's where we differ. I think there's a lot you can tell us, Danny. First off, you can tell me about the guns."

Newt folded his arms. "No comment."

"It's a serious offence, being in possession of a firearm, not to mention threatening folk with it."

"Get lost."

"Who's behind setting up that building belonging to Buckley's to produce the drugs?"

"No comment."

Calladine sighed. This would get them nowhere. "Who are you afraid of?"

"Not scared of owt."

"Yes you are, otherwise you'd talk to me. We've arrested the six people we found working in that building. They will be shown a photo of you. Recognise it, will they Danny?"

The young man scowled.

"I don't think you realise the trouble you're in, Danny. I can help you. Answer our questions, tell us who is really behind this, and it'll go better for your case."

"You talking a deal?" There was a flicker of interest. Then it was gone.

"We'll see," Calladine said. "That would depend on what you tell us, and how useful it is."

"Piss off, copper. Talk to you and I'm dead."

Calladine nodded. "Very powerful then, this big boss you're terrified of."

"Didn't say I was scared, did I? I don't grass is all."

"If it was him in that chair, do you imagine he wouldn't grass on you?"

"You might as well give up, 'cause I've got nowt to say."

"Okay. Have it your way. In that case you'll be staying with us a bit longer. We'll keep having these talks. Sooner or later you're going to tell me what I want to hear. When you're ready to talk to me properly, just call out."

Calladine and Rocco made their way back to the incident room. "Isn't there any intelligence on the streets about who this new Mr Big is?" Calladine asked.

Rocco shook his head. "No. It's all news to us. Whoever he is, he's moved in and taken over, all under the radar."

"There has to be something, perhaps a whisper we've missed. Do we have anyone who could find out?"

"I know a bloke in the Wheatsheaf who fancies himself as an informant. I've been softening him up for a month or two, buying him the odd pint, passing the time of day. Reckons he keeps his ear to the ground. I could have a word. Mind you, he's not come up with anything useful yet."

"Do that, Rocco. We need to wrap this up. The drugs are one thing, but we've still got two murders to deal with."

"I need a word about that, sir," Rocco said.

As soon as they entered the incident room, Alice called out to them. "Something odd. Keith Wrigley is downstairs. You know, the ex-prisoner who was pally with Norbury. He's come in of his own volition and has asked to speak to someone who worked the Norbury case."

"Ford can't do it, he's at Oldston, so that'll be me then." Calladine sighed.

"Before you go and see him," Rocco said, "I need to tell you something. That phone data I've been studying. Both Ingrid Plesec and Eve Buckley have the same number on their mobiles. It's a pay-as-you-go, untraceable. It was used to ring Ingrid once, the night her sister said she went out to the cleaning job and never came back. But it's been used to ring Eve Buckley several times over the past couple of weeks. There's a number of texts too."

About to go out, Calladine stopped. That didn't make any sense. "Are you sure, Rocco? This could be crucial."

"Yep. See for yourself." Rocco handed him the printout.

Calladine crosschecked the two numbers. Rocco was right, they matched. "That means the killings and the drugs are linked somehow." He looked around at the team. "I have no idea what this means. Put those thinking caps on, folks. See if you can work out what we're looking at. Meanwhile, I'll go and have a word with the joker downstairs. We'll discuss this when I get back. Rocco, have that word with your mate in the pub."

* * *

Calladine entered the small interview room. The central heating was on full blast, and Wrigley stank to high heaven. He'd evidently not been near water in weeks.

"Where have you been, Keith? You've caused a lot of bother, you know. Police the length and breadth of the North West have been searching for you. Why abscond?"

Wrigley smiled. "I promised George, you see. He died not long after I got out. When I read about it, it made me think. I had to do what he asked."

"What did you promise him?" Calladine asked.

"He told me he didn't kill that woman. Someone set him up."

Why would Wrigley lie? "Did he tell you who?"

Wrigley shook his head. "He wouldn't say. He was too frightened. He said that if he told me, my life would be at

186

risk too. The real killer's powerful, and would have got to us both. George didn't feel safe even in prison."

"I appreciate your trying to help, Keith, but without a name there isn't much I can do. Did he tell you anything at all?"

"Whoever set him up fixed the evidence so as not to incriminate himself."

Calladine shook his head. "That isn't likely. Access to evidence collected in a murder case is restricted, and everything is logged and checked."

"This man removed a contact lens that was found on one of the bodies. George said it must have had the real killer's DNA on it."

Chapter 32

It was not yet five in the afternoon, but Rocco's informant was already propping up the bar at the Wheatsheaf. Rocco bought a pint and stood next to him. Alf Crawford was a waster who divided his time between the pub and the betting shop. But he heard a lot of stuff, spoke to people.

Alf proffered his money to the barman for his next pint.

Rocco smiled at him. "Let me get this. Busy day?"

"No, lad. Been catching up on me sleep. You?" Alf said.

"No time to sleep, Alf. We've got a heavy case on the go. He mouthed the word 'drugs.'

"That'll be t'Hobfield. I heard. Stupid kids, doing what that bastard tells 'em to."

"What bastard, Alf?"

"Newt and his cronies. You've taken him in, word 'as it."

Rocco hoped Alf would say something more useful. "In my opinion, that lad's not smart enough to run an operation like that. What d'you think? He doesn't look the part either. Scruffy bugger, isn't he?"

Alf nodded. "S'pose you're right. After all he got caught, and that's not clever."

"Mark my words, there'll be a man with a brain and money at the back of him. Pushing buttons and organising everything from behind a desk." Rocco looked at Alf expectantly. "Any ideas, Alf? Who d'you reckon that might be?"

"I've seen him getting into Miles Erskine's car a couple of times. I did wonder. I just reckoned Erskine was buying dope off him like everyone else. But I was surprised. A man like that, at the top of his game."

That was a name Rocco hadn't expected to hear. Miles Erskine was a local businessman, who owned a construction firm. In the Leesdon area, whoever wasn't employed by Buckley's Pharmaceuticals probably worked at Erskine's.

"What made you think it was Erskine?" Rocco asked.

"Looked like his car. Brand new merc. Tinted windows, the lot."

"Can't be him," Rocco said. "He's worth a mint. Why would he bother? He can't need the money."

Alf shrugged. "I don't know. But construction has taken a dip. They've been laying folk off. Erskine didn't get that mill refurbishment he was counting on. A neighbour of mine has worked at Erskine's for twenty years or more. Got sacked last week."

"Didn't realise. I'll keep it in mind. Have another one, Alf."

* * *

An hour later, Calladine met the team for a briefing. "Keith Wrigley told me that Norbury is innocent, and that the real killer tampered with evidence. Apparently, a contact lens found on one of the bodies was removed."

Ruth shook her head. "That can't happen. He's talking rubbish."

"That would depend on who removed it," Calladine said. "Back in the days before the Duggan, evidence used to be stored at the nick investigating the case. We had an evidence store here at Leesdon. It's now part of the archive. This contact lens would have been stored at Oldston. It is possible that it could have been taken."

"That would mean a policeman or a SOCO," Ruth said.

"There are admin staff too," Calladine added.

"I've been looking through the case files, and I didn't see anything," Alice said. "There was definitely no contact lens."

Ruth nodded. "We've all looked."

"Nevertheless, we'll have to follow it up. I'll have a word with Ford. He might recall something. Doc Hoyle was the pathologist at the time. He might be able to help too." He looked at Rocco. "Speak to your friend?"

"Yes. He mentioned Miles Erskine. Newton has been seen getting into his car a couple of times. A big posh job, a merc. Might be nothing, but you never know."

Calladine hadn't expected this name to come up. "Erskine? If he really is a bona fide businessman, why mix with the likes of Newton?"

"That's what I thought. Alf reckons he could have been buying drugs, but I don't think that was it. A man like him is unlikely to be buying them on the Hobfield."

"We'll speak to Newton again shortly."

Calladine looked around the room. Now for the hard bit. He'd told Ruth, and now it was time to come clean to the others about Eve's part in all this. "The drugs were produced in a building belonging to Eve Buckley's factory. It's the old, dilapidated one further up the hill. Buckley's don't use it anymore. They kidnapped me and threatened Eve that my continued safety depended on her silence. It worked. She did exactly what they told her. That included putting the money into my bank account."

They all gasped.

"But she's your mother!" Joyce exclaimed.

Calladine shrugged. "She had no choice. What was she supposed to do? If she told you lot, there was every chance I'd never be seen again."

"Her brother's a former superintendent," Rocco said. "Couldn't she have got him on board?"

"Eve was terrified. She has other family apart from me."

But Calladine could see they weren't convinced. "This is where the case gets complicated," he said. "Eve was always contacted by phone, and she never met anyone in person. Rocco has discovered that all the calls she got were from the same pay-as-you-go as the one used to call Ingrid Plesec on the night she was killed."

Ruth stared at him. "The two cases are linked? The killings? The drugs? But how can that be? The crimes are so different. Apart from the phone number, there's no other link, right? Are you sure about this?"

"Yes. I'm hoping that the 'hows' and the 'whys' become clearer as we get more evidence. Rocco and I will have another word with Danny Newton. After him, we'll speak to Flake again. Ruth, speak to Alenka. Ask her about Erskine. Has she ever seen him and Newton together? Or even heard the name? Alice, look again at the evidence log for the Norbury killings. Given what we've been told, you might spot something new."

Calladine added the new information to the incident board. "I suppose I'll have to speak to Birch, and bring her up to speed. She isn't going to believe it."

"I'm still wondering, why you?" Ruth said. "The kidnapping, I mean."

He shrugged. "Because of my connection with Eve."

"Like you pointed out, Eve has other family. And if you don't mind me saying, she's more emotionally attached to them. Her grandson, for example. You have to consider that you were taken because of the Norbury case. You worked it. These recent killings would have been familiar to you. You'd have remembered. With you out of the way, that doesn't happen."

"But it did."

"Only because of Alice and her obsession with the archive and your old cases."

Ruth was right. "Are you suggesting there's another link, not Eve?" he asked.

"Yes, I am," she said. "Think about it. The killings and the drugs."

"So, who are we looking for?"

She frowned. "That's the biggy. I'll have to think about that one."

"Are you free tomorrow night?"

Ruth looked a little surprised. "Don't know, why?"

"Eve is hosting a do at the Leesworth Hall Hotel. She's invited me and Layla, but I think it might be a better idea to take you along."

"I'm flattered! But why?"

Calladine smiled. "Because chances are, Miles Erskine will be there. Do no harm to get to know him better. He's a complete unknown to us."

"Okay, it's a date. Formal, is it?"

"Afraid so."

"Won't Layla mind?" Ruth asked.

"She'll be working anyway. Grabs all the overtime she can, that one."

Chapter 33

By the time Ruth got to the Hobfield, it was beginning to get dark. After all the excitement earlier, there were few people about. She went into Heron House and climbed the stairs up to the first floor.

She knocked at the door to Alenka's flat. "Who is it?" Alenka called out, her voice shaky. Not surprising, after what had happened earlier.

"It's Ruth. Can we talk?"

Alenka opened the door, cradling Lara in her arms.

"I'm afraid to put her down after Newt and what he did. If you hadn't come, if your inspector hadn't talked Newt down, things could have turned out very differently."

"Newt's in custody. He won't be bothering anyone for a while. Do you mind answering some questions?" Ruth asked.

They went in and sat down.

"Was it him who killed Ingrid?"

"We don't think so," Ruth replied

"I can't believe that she is really gone. That I'll never see her again. I know she had her faults but she was my sister and I miss her."

The young woman was tearful. "Tell me about Danny Newton. We need him to help us if we are to find Ingrid's killer. The more we know about him, the better."

"He made me work for him," Alenka said. "If I refused, he threatened to hurt Lara. Plus, he knew about Ingrid and what I'd done."

"Do you know who Newt worked for? Did he ever mention any names? Did he ever have anyone with him who didn't live on the estate?"

"Newt was always very careful. He never mentioned names. He called the man who ran the operation the 'big boss.' I got the impression it was a secret, and if he said anything, he'd be in trouble."

"Did you ever see this man?" Ruth asked.

"Not the man. But he had a big car with tinted windows. He had a driver too. The car was black, a Mercedes, this year's model."

"You didn't catch sight of the registration number, I suppose?" Ruth wasn't hopeful.

"I took a photo with my mobile. I was curious about this 'big boss' Newt worked for." Alenka scrolled through the images on her phone. "Here. This is it."

Right enough, a black merc. Unfortunately Alenka hadn't captured the whole plate but it began with the letters 'MTE.'

"Text it to me, please. Thank you. You did well." Ruth cast her eye around the room. The girl didn't have much. "I'm afraid we'll have to take a statement about what happened earlier. One of my colleagues will come round. Just tell him the truth. It will go better for you in the end."

Alenka turned wide, frightened eyes on Ruth. "I won't. I've broken the law. I'll be punished, and they'll take Lara away from me."

"It's your first offence. You were coerced. You are Lara's auntie and she's settled and happy with you. I'm sure the courts will be fair."

Ruth left Alenka sitting with Lara, aware that there was every possibility she'd be charged with drug dealing. No need to rub her nose in it tonight, though. She'd had a bad day.

* * *

"Right, Danny. Time to get serious." Calladine said. He and Rocco sat facing Danny 'Newt' Newton.

"Not in the mood, copper. It's getting late. I've got stuff to do."

"Unless you speak to me, Danny, you'll be with us even longer. What's the rush anyway? Mr Erskine expecting you, is he?"

That did it. Newt's face turned white. His eyes darted from one of them to the other. "Who've you been talking to?"

"Just people. You see, Danny, your meetings with Erskine weren't as private as you both thought. Leesdon's a small place, and there are eyes and ears everywhere."

"It's got nowt do with him. I don't know what you're on about."

"Let me get this straight. You're prepared to take the rap for the drugs, kidnap, the attempted murder of a colleague of mine and recent murders of two young women." Calladine counted them off on his fingers.

Newt's mouth dropped open. "I haven't killed anyone! You can't pin owt like that on me. I might've sold a few pills around the estate, but that's it."

"That's not good enough. You see, the crimes are linked. You knew about my kidnap, but more importantly, you knew one of the murder victims. Come on, Danny, it's time to talk to us."

Newt started to bluster, his previous bravado all gone. "I can't. That is . . . I need to think. Have you spoken to

Flake? Yeah, go and talk to him! Let him take some of the heat off me."

"You still don't want to talk about Erskine?"

Newt sat back. "Don't know the man."

* * *

"The name Erskine rattled him alright," Rocco said. "Alf was on the nose there." They were on their way back to the incident room.

Calladine shook his head. "We haven't got enough though, have we? We can't even approach the man. He's a pillar of the community. One way or another, we need to get more."

"So what now?"

Calladine looked up at the office clock. "We'll call it a day, Rocco. It's late — again. We'll pick it up in the morning."

Alice was still at her desk, head down, engrossed in a pile of documents.

"Found anything?" Calladine called to her.

"Not yet, sir."

"Leave it now. We've done enough for today."

She nodded, and smiled at Rocco. "Fancy going for a drink?"

Calladine gave him a nudge in the back. "Well, don't keep the young lady waiting."

Calladine gathered his stuff together. He was on foot again. A brisk ten minute walk through the side streets, and he'd be home.

He was turning into his own street when he heard the footsteps behind him. Oh no, he thought, not again.

He was about to react when the man behind him spoke.

"Don't turn round. Listen carefully. You will drop the charge against Newton. He will be released. Do this, and your family and that cute little kiddie will stay safe. Refuse, and you can start saying your goodbyes."

Calladine had heard enough. He'd been caught like this once before, and he wasn't going to let it happen again. He spun around, just in time to see a tall, thin figure legging it back down the street. The man was youngish, he guessed, and dressed in dark clothing. Moments later, he'd turned the corner and was gone. Calladine tried to place the voice. Gruff. Northern accent, and he'd cleared his throat a couple of times. A smoker, perhaps?

He took out his mobile and rang the station. Birch had long since gone home, so he left a message on her answerphone. He also alerted the desk sergeant. He wanted the watch on Harry Ireson beefed up.

Chapter 34

Day 7

After a sleepless night, Calladine went into the station early the next morning.

"We've got the CCTV footage from the hospital through," Rocco said. "I've had a look, but I can't make up my mind. It was dark, and raining. The killer chose his spot well. The light was out in that section of the car park, so the video is full of shadows."

"See if the tech boys can clean it up," Calladine said. "This case has gone on long enough. We're making no headway at all."

"At least we now know that the two cases are linked somehow," Ruth said. "And that link has something to do with you."

"You may be wrong."

"You had to be got out of the way for some reason. Knowing the details of the Norbury case would do it," she said.

He shrugged. "I don't see why. All I recall is a few disjointed facts. That's no reason to drag me off and keep me prisoner."

"This case is complicated. It's a real puzzle, and you're in there somewhere," Ruth said.

"Inspector Calladine! Are you alright? Not hurt again, I hope." DCI Birch entered the incident room. "I've just listened to your message — very worrying. The kidnappers have obviously not given up. How are your family doing?"

"I've asked for increased monitoring of Eve Buckley's house, and for Ruth's Harry. As for the others — Zoe, my daughter is on holiday, and the rest of the Buckley family, I can hardly lock them all away."

"Tell them to be careful," she said and turned to leave.

"Want to tell us what happened?" Ruth wasn't about to be fobbed off. She had that look on her face. "Has Harry been threatened again. You should have told me straight away."

Calladine sighed. "Someone came up behind me on my street last night and warned me off. Told me to drop the charges against Newton."

"I'm betting there was an *or else*. There was, wasn't there?" She stared at him.

"He threatened my family as well this time."

"And you have no idea who it was?"

He shook his head. "No. I only caught a glimpse of him running away."

"Do we speak to Newton again?" Rocco asked.

"We'll have another go at Flake this morning. A night in the cells might have loosened his tongue."

"Sir!" Alice looked up from her desk. "I think I might have found something. There is an entry in the evidence log that looks a bit suspect. I've been sitting here trying to decide if it's been altered in some way." She handed the book to Calladine. "The entry dated the fifth. See?"

The entry was handwritten in ink, an untidy scrawl.

"I can't even make out the signature," said Calladine. "It looks to me as if it's been partly erased and overwritten."

"That's what I thought. I can't make out what the listed item was, either. But it could be the contact lens."

Calladine squinted at the entry from all angles, but he couldn't make it out. "Julian might be able to help. Failing him, try the tech boys again." He handed it back to Alice. "Get it sorted as soon as. We need the information quickly."

"If someone on the Norbury case did tamper with evidence, what then?" asked Ruth. "What does it even mean?"

"I have no idea. Let's see if we can get this cleaned up first."

* * *

Calladine and Rocco sat opposite Andy Prior — Flake, as he was known on the streets.

"We've got your mate worried," Calladine said. "I think we know the name of his big boss."

Flake shrugged. "So?"

"Terrified of the man, isn't he? The boss finds out, he'll be coming after him. You too, just to make sure."

"You're bluffing, trying to scare me. Well, I've no idea who Newt's boss is. He never told me. Reckoned he couldn't."

"Liked his privacy, didn't he, this big man. Why do you reckon that was, Flake?"

He shrugged again.

Calladine leaned forward. "I think it was because he didn't want anyone to know his identity. I think this big boss is someone we'd all recognise. And he doesn't want that. He wants his reputation to stay squeaky clean. Anything goes wrong, he's got the likes of you and Newt to take what's coming."

"I've done nothing. I don't see why I should take the blame. You have to let me go."

"You'll be charged, Andy. You're guilty of manufacturing drugs, being party to a kidnap, plus a list of other stuff. We can only help you if you help us. First, tell me about the guns."

Flake appeared to wrestle with this. Eventually, he sighed. "You'll have to protect me, even inside. It won't be safe for me anywhere if I talk to you."

Calladine nodded.

"Newt got them from his boss and gave them out. Dane Hamilton must have got one, and that silly sod, Henry Johns. Newt gave him one for a laugh."

"And you? Do you have one?"

"No. All I've done is deal the drugs. Newt told me to watch that factory up in the hills. But everything was okay. There was no need to hang around."

"Do you have any idea who Newt's boss is?" Calladine said. "It's important. If we are to stop this, we need to know."

"He wouldn't tell me. Said I was safer that way. But from the car he drove, I'd say he had money."

"Do you know who injured my colleague? Someone drove a car at him. He's got serious injuries."

The lad hung his head. "Not me. That was down to Newt. It was supposed to keep you lot busy while the drugs job was going on. He torched the car and dumped it by the reservoir."

* * *

Calladine and Rocco walked back down the corridor. "We'll give Newton a little longer to stew, and then we'll have another go at him," Calladine said. "Once he knows Flake's spoken to us, he might see sense. And get uniform up the reservoir. They should find the car that hit Long up there. It was burnt out, but you never know, forensics might still give us something. Right now, I need a lever to use on Danny Newton."

Ruth looked up from her computer. "While you two were interviewing, I took the liberty of looking a little closer at Erskine's business," she said. "It *is* in trouble. Miles Erskine has taken out a couple of large bank loans recently. He's made his backers nervous."

"Where are his offices?" Calladine asked.

"The industrial park off the bypass, between here and Oldston. His firm built the place some years ago. Back then, his business was booming." Ruth picked up a sheaf of documents. "I've got the latest company financial report and some newspaper clippings."

Calladine leafed through them. He'd never met Erskine and had no idea what he even looked like. "This him? The bloke in the expensive suit?"

Ruth nodded. "The others are members of his board. I've done a quick check on the names and all of them are spotless. The woman standing next to Erskine is his accountant. She's also a member of Erskine Construction's board of directors, and a friend of his."

Calladine stared at the image. He could hardly believe his eyes. "I know this woman, Ruth. I've met her recently."

"She's local. Says there she lives in Lowermill."

Calladine shook his head, frowning. "That's not where I met her. We met in Scotland, at Moortop Manse. She was the woman who was supposed to look after me. I remember her distinctive eyes."

Ruth looked at him and grinned. "This is our way in! It gives us our reason to go round there and start digging."

Calladine was already writing names on the incident board. The woman was called Joanna Fox. She and Erskine were now persons of interest.

Chapter 35

"Want me to come with you?" Ruth asked.

"No. You're coming with me tonight. The chances are both Erskine and this woman will be there, so we'll keep you in the background for now. I'll take Rocco. In the meantime, find out all you can about Miles Erskine. His background, where his money came from, and his family life. Do it fast, and dig deep. I want the dirt."

This was indeed a breakthrough. There was now every chance that they'd be able to apprehend the woman who'd been party to his kidnapping and imprisonment in Scotland.

Calladine and Rocco set out for Erskine's.

"So, what's our reason for seeing them?" Rocco asked.

"Initially, I want to speak to Joanna Fox. I'm also going to ask Erskine if he knows Newton."

"This is all very well," said Rocco, "but it's all about the drugs. That's important, yes, but aren't we in danger of allowing the murders to take a back seat?"

Rocco had a point. Julian hadn't got back to them about the DNA yet, and there was still the CCTV to wade through. The fact of the matter was, Calladine was fearful for his family's safety. Somewhere down the line, the two cases were linked. He had to hope that the connection would soon reveal itself."

"Could Erskine be our killer?" Rocco said. "That would fit, wouldn't it? He was around back then, when the first murders took place. He was wealthy, powerful. He'd have known people who could sort things for him."

"You're talking the missing evidence?" Calladine said.

"That and the possible fitting up of Norbury."

Calladine would have to think about that one. But he wasn't dismissing it out of hand. From where they were with the case at the moment, Erskine was ideally placed.

The receptionist was cool. In fact she was icy. "You should have made an appointment. Mr Erskine doesn't see people without one."

"He'll see us." Calladine smiled at her and showed his badge. "Now ring his office and tell him we're here."

Reluctantly, she did as she was told. Minutes later, the two detectives were gliding up to the top floor in a padded lift.

Miles Erskine was sitting at his desk. He gestured to two chairs facing him. "Sit down, gentlemen. Tell me, what can I do for you?"

He was all smiles, charming, geared to impress, from the vast office to the tailored suit and smooth manners. Erskine was in his late fifties. His hair was dark, just showing the first signs of greying at the temples. He was a tall, well-built man who obviously kept himself in shape. He certainly looked the part of a successful businessman.

Calladine took a seat. "A couple of things. Do you know a young man called Danny Newton?"

"No, I don't believe I do. Why? Should I?" His gaze was steady. Not a flicker.

"That depends, Mr Erskine. We currently have him in custody. So far, he hasn't mentioned you, but others have.

Some of them think the two of you have a business arrangement. It's that arrangement that interests me."

Erskine laughed. "I don't recognise the name, so there's no *arrangement*, as you put it. Whoever's been talking to you has got it wrong. Why do you ask?"

Calladine smiled broadly. "Call it a hunch." He took the newspaper clipping from his pocket. "Do you know this woman?"

"You know I do," Erskine said. "It's plain enough in the article. Joanna is a member of my board. She works in this very building."

"Is she around?"

"Joanna is an accountant. Her office is on the floor below this one."

Calladine turned to Rocco, sitting quietly beside him. "Would you mind asking her to join us?"

Erskine didn't look quite so affable anymore. "What's this all about? Exactly what do you think we've done?"

His tone gave him away. He was angry now. If they hadn't been police, Calladine was in no doubt that he'd have had them thrown out.

"I'm busy compiling a list of certain misdemeanours," Calladine said, "top of which at the moment, as far as you and Ms Fox are concerned, is kidnap and drug dealing. Dealing on a large scale, I should add. That means the entire process, from manufacture to the selling of the stuff on the streets. But that's not all. I'm also looking into an attempted murder and two other killings."

Erskine stood up. "You're mad! You have some nerve, coming in here and spouting this rubbish. What proof do you have?"

Calladine smiled. "None at all." He was goading the man. "But I'm sure that'll change pretty soon. I wonder how Newton will feel when he's taking the rap for your crimes too? I bet he doesn't stay quiet for long."

"I want you to leave now, or I'll call security. You're not welcome here now, or at any time in the future. You can't come in here and fling these imaginary accusations at me!"

The office door opened and Joanna Fox entered, followed by Rocco. When she spotted Calladine, she gasped, and tried to turn back. Rocco blocked her path.

Calladine nodded at her. "We meet again. Hope your journey back from Ullapool wasn't as tedious as mine."

"I, I don't know what you mean," she stammered.

"What is this about, Inspector? What do you think Joanna has done?" Erskine asked.

"She was party to a kidnapping. That kidnapping involved a certain amount of violence. And I was the victim."

Erskine laughed again, shaking his head. "I hardly think that is probable."

"You're wrong. The house I was taken to will provide all the proof we need. Ms Fox's DNA, as well as mine, will be all over the place." He turned to her with a smile. "You do yourself no favours if you choose to deny your part in this."

"Miles! You can't let this happen."

"I'm afraid he has no choice in the matter," Calladine said. "You, Ms Fox, are coming down to the station with us. We want you to answer some questions."

"Miles? Get me a solicitor! Someone who knows his stuff." She looked at Calladine. "I don't know how you found me, but it won't get you anywhere."

"That's where we differ. I happen to think it will," Calladine said.

"Joanna is right. You're wasting your time. I'll have her out before the end of the day," Erskine said.

"We'll see. Rocco, escort Ms Fox down to the car."

Calladine turned to Erskine. "Should you decide to see reason, and want to talk to me, here's my card." He tossed it onto the gleaming desk.

* * *

As soon as they were back at the station, Calladine went for a word with Rhona Birch and told her where things stood.

"Given it was me who was kidnapped, I can't interview the woman. Her solicitor would have us on that one. Joanna Fox is a tough cookie. She won't simply roll over and tell us the truth, so we need a really seasoned interrogator. We also need the results from the forensic team that examined that house. Once we have proper evidence, we'll have got her. Whether she confesses or not, the CPS will agree to prosecute."

"Okay," Birch said, "I'll speak to her myself. I'll do the interview with DC Rockliffe. I'll get onto the station in Ullapool and get them to email me the report pronto. We will need a sample of Joanna Fox's DNA to cross match. What did you make of Erskine?"

"I got the impression he rules his domain with an iron fist, so much so that no one'll say anything against him. Newton is terrified of him. Even locked up in prison, Norbury went in fear of his life. If Erskine is at the bottom of this, he has some reach."

Chapter 36

"The man's a mystery," Ruth said. She swivelled her office chair round to face Joyce. "I've been sitting at this computer for over an hour, and what have I discovered about Erskine? A big fat nothing. Other than that he's self-made, and dragged himself up from poverty, which we knew anyway."

Joyce smiled. "Where's Alice when you need her?"

Ruth checked her watch. "She's gone to the Duggan and then she's going to find Doc Hoyle. See if he can recall anything about the missing contact lens she's been going on about."

"DI Calladine?"

"He's earwigging on the interview. Birch is taking Joanna Fox to task over the kidnapping. Rocco's in with her. Tom can't get involved, since he was the victim."

"Doesn't Erskine have a family?" Joyce said. "Isn't there a marriage registered somewhere?"

"Not as far as I can see. Which is odd, don't you think? A man like him, purporting to be your model upstanding citizen. You'd expect a glamorous wife, and kids."

"Mr Mystery then. You've got your work cut out."

Ruth turned back to her computer. She couldn't believe there was nothing at all out there about this man. "I'd wondered about a name change, but I've found his birth certificate. He was born in Oldston. No siblings. That's about the lot though. Hang on a minute. What's this?" Ruth was looking at an old police record she'd found. "Aha! He was a known associate of Ray Fallon's. Now we're getting somewhere. Erskine was never arrested or even cautioned, but he was close to Fallon for a long while. They don't say what the nature of that relationship was."

"DI Calladine might have something to suggest in that case," Joyce said. "Isn't Fallon's wife doing time in prison?"

Calladine came into the incident room. He wasn't looking happy. "Joanna Fox has admitted being at the house in Scotland."

"That's good, isn't it?" Ruth said. "It means you've got her."

"She played it very cool. Said she had no idea what was going on, just that she'd been asked to keep house and look after me for a few days. Joanna Fox reckons she was threatened like I was. She did say she was very well paid for her time, but she has no idea who by! The bloody woman didn't mention Erskine once."

"That can't be right. She's playing games. She knows who sent her up there alright. I'm surprised Birch didn't get more out of her."

"It wasn't for want of trying, Ruth. But Fox had a solicitor who was as sharp as a razor."

"What now?" Ruth asked.

"She's been charged with kidnapping. The victim, yours truly. Let's see her wriggle out of that. Given time to consider her position, she may decide to tell us about Erskine."

"I've been trying to find out about Erskine," Ruth said. "There's precious little, no family details or anything. But there is one glimmer of hope."

"Go on."

"He was an associate of Ray Fallon's. Apparently they were pretty close at one time."

"Ray Fallon is dead, Ruth, as well you know."

"I thought you might have a word with Marilyn, see if she remembers Erskine. If she does, she'll help you. I'd say Marilyn Fallon is someone who's not afraid of anything or anyone."

* * *

Alice followed Julian Batho into his lab.

"I'm afraid we've been pushed for time," he said. "I'm working flat out on what we have. It's labour intensive work going through the rubbish from the first site. The fragment of flesh found at the second site is being tested as we speak, but it'll take time to get the DNA results through."

Alice winced. At least Kelly Donald had put up a fight. Just thinking about what those women must have gone through made her feel sick. Alice felt sorry for Julian. He looked very sombre. She knew a little of the story of him and DC Imogen Goode. They would have been married now if she hadn't been brutally murdered. Julian had never really gotten over it. He coped with his grief by working himself into the ground.

"Did you find anything else of interest on the second body?"

He shook his head. "Apart from the pregnancy, nothing."

"I'll leave you to it. I'll just have a word with Doc Hoyle and then I can call it a day."

But it was proving difficult to find him. She wanted to speak to him about the contact lens, the evidence that had gone missing at the time of the Norbury case. She'd phoned his house, but he wasn't home, nor was he at the surgery where he worked part time. She decided to try the hospital.

Leesdon Infirmary was still very busy. A number of the folk who'd taken the new drugs had had bad reactions. Doc Hoyle was there, but in A&E, and up to his eyes in it.

"Can I have a word?" Alice asked.

"It'll have to be quick. We have an ambulance on the way in from a road traffic accident."

"Do you remember the Norbury case? It was twenty years ago, and a woman was horrifically murdered."

"I've dealt with hundreds of murders over the years, but I do vaguely remember that one. Tom talked about it recently. It was back in the days before the Duggan. There isn't a lot I can tell you off the top of my head, particularly at the moment. Look, when I get home later, I'll dig out my notes and ring you. Why are you interested? Is it the current killings?"

"Yes. They are like that one in every detail. What I'm interested in is any anomalies you may have made a note of."

"Okay then. We'll speak later."

It was something at least. Alice thanked him.

Chapter 37

Calladine phoned the prison in West Yorkshire where Marilyn Fallon was being held and arranged to see her urgently.

"It'll take me about an hour to get there," he told the team. He checked his watch. "Traffic'll be bad on the way home, but I should make it before six. I'll give you the feedback then." He noticed Alice's empty desk. "Where is she?"

"Doing some research," said Ruth. "She went to have a chat with Julian and then she was going to talk to Doc Hoyle about the contact lens that went missing."

"Fine," said Calladine. "You two carry on with the research into Erskine. I find it hard to believe that there's nothing at all."

"Well, I've looked thoroughly," Ruth said. "He's been very careful not to leave a trail. No social media, no marriage, no mentions in the papers — nothing."

It was down to Marilyn Fallon then, and whatever she could tell him about friend Erskine. She might not be pleased to see him. Calladine had told her he'd visit regularly, but he hadn't kept his promise. She could be forgiven for being put out. But then again, he had taken on her dog, Sam. He'd become so fond of the mutt that he'd almost forgotten it once belonged to Marilyn and Ray. Marilyn had doted on that dog. He had plenty of photos on his mobile, so hopefully a look at them and she'd soften pretty soon.

As he drove, Calladine tried to work out what might have brought Ray and Erskine together. If it had been villainy, why had Erskine walked away scot free? Yet another piece of the puzzle he needed to fit in.

* * *

The female guard ignored his greeting. "We'd have appreciated a little more notice. Marilyn's a quiet woman, keeps herself to herself. She was in two minds whether to see you or not. On the other hand, she doesn't get many visitors. This might do her good."

Calladine was shown into a small visitor's room, where Marilyn Fallon sat alone at a table.

"Tom! You came — finally."

She looked gaunt and pale, nothing like her old self. The Marilyn he remembered always looked as if she'd just been to the hairdresser. Perfect make-up and designer clothes were her thing. This woman looked her age. She was stooped, as if she carried all the cares of the world on her shoulders.

"Sorry, Marilyn. Work. You know how it is."

"I know how *you* are." She smiled. "How is my Sam? I hope you're taking good care of him?"

"He wants for nothing. I have a new woman in my life — Layla. She dotes on him as much as you used to. He spends a lot of time with her when I'm at work." He took out his mobile and showed her the images. "That's Layla with Sam. See how they are together."

He handed her the phone and watched as she scrolled through the pictures. A smile lit up her face.

"Another dog lover, like that lovely Lydia you used to go out with."

Calladine wondered if Marilyn knew that Ray had had Lydia killed. Well, he wouldn't push it. It was history now.

"Thank you for taking care of Sam. He was the one thing I could rely on in those days." She sighed and handed back the phone. "So what do you want? I'm not stupid enough to believe that you've just come to say hello."

"I've come to ask you about an old friend of Ray's."

"Not so loud, Tom. The women in here know what I did. I've had a lot of trouble, and I don't want it all dragging up again. I've been beaten up twice, you know."

Calladine was puzzled. "They won't even have known Ray!"

"He was a gangster. Plenty of the women in here have menfolk who knew him. Believe me, my name was mud for a long time. I did kill him, or have you forgotten?"

He hadn't. "Granted, it wasn't all that clever, but nonetheless it was very brave of you."

"Brave? Stupid, more like. He was on remand and I poisoned him. I should have thought it through. I don't know what possessed me."

"You'd had enough, simple as that."

"Anyway, how can I help?"

"Do you remember a man called Miles Erskine?" Calladine asked.

Marilyn laughed. "Erskine. He's trouble, I remember that. I dislike that man intensely. He's a creep, even Ray said so. They did some business together from time to time. Ray tolerated him, said he was useful, but he didn't trust him one inch. He always reckoned that one day, Miles would drop him in it."

"So, Erskine is a villain?"

"Oh yes. Very low-key. Works quietly in the shadows, has that businessman front so no one suspects him. But Erskine's a crook through and through."

"Has he ever killed anyone?" Calladine was thinking about the murders.

"Possibly, but you'll never prove it. He keeps his hands spotless. Then, of course, there's his ace in the hole." Marilyn smiled knowingly.

"What do you mean?"

"His partner."

Calladine stared at her. "We've done our research, and we can't find a single trace of a wife or any other woman in his life."

"You won't. He isn't married, and his long-term partner is a man."

Calladine wasn't expecting that. "Erskine is gay?"

"Yes, which is why Ray didn't like him." She laughed. "You know what Ray was like, didn't understand anything different from what he called 'normal.'"

"I don't understand. I had no idea that Erskine was gay."

"You didn't need to. You didn't know Erskine back then, but you did know his partner. He was in CID, same as you. He wouldn't have wanted you to know he was in a same-sex relationship, and particularly not with Erskine. No reason you should."

"Who is this partner?"

"I don't have a proper name. But you must know him, Tom. Ray got his nickname from you. You called him 'Angry' — remember? He had a short fuse. Nothing was ever right. He blamed everyone but himself when things went wrong. He got on everyone's nerves, particularly yours. The reason you transferred from Oldston to Leesdon was partly because of him."

"*Angry?*" Gradually it began to come back to him. He'd completely forgotten. He could have kicked himself. He knew very well who Marilyn was talking about. If she was right, then they had a serious problem on their hands. "Are you sure?"

"They've been together for years. Whoever he is, he still holds a top position. He must do, he's saved Erskine's bacon on more than one occasion. Erskine used to piss Ray off, always boasting about his pet policeman. He said Ray had one of his own in the family, and was an idiot for not taking advantage of it."

Calladine felt sick. This was much worse than he'd imagined. "I need to go." He leaned across the table and kissed her cheek. "You've helped a lot, Marilyn. Thank you."

Chapter 38

It was gone six p.m. when Calladine got back to the nick, but the team were still there, all busy working.

Ruth looked up from her desk. "I hope you've got more than we have."

Calladine nodded. "Marilyn was a great help. She told me stuff I never knew, and reminded me of things I'd completely forgotten. First off, Miles Erskine is gay. I wasn't aware of that because Ray never told me, and I didn't know Erskine back then. What's more important though, is that his long-term partner is a member of the force. Over the years, he's helped Erskine escape justice numerous times."

The team looked shocked. "Do we know him?" Ruth asked.

"Yes, we do. But for the time being, I don't want to say anything. It's sensitive information, and I need cast-iron proof before I start throwing accusations about."

"You think Erskine is responsible for what? The drugs, the kidnapping? The murders too?" Ruth said.

"Given that he's being shielded, and has always had someone to watch his back, that's a strong possibility. We do have that phone number. It connects the drugs to the murders."

"Do you have any idea in what way Erskine was protected?" Ruth asked. "Alice asked Doc Hoyle about the lens, and he's going to check his records when he gets home. That could be a case in point."

"If our killer is Erskine," Rocco said, "then whoever took the lens could be your mysterious member of the police force."

Calladine nodded. "That's what I was thinking."

"Do we have enough to tackle Erskine about any of this?" Rocco asked.

"No. A few short texts that said very little. Besides, we've already tried that, Rocco. We need Newton to talk to us. Is he still in the cells?" Calladine asked.

"Yep, shouting his head off and making a thorough nuisance of himself." Rocco grinned.

"Alenka Plesec was only able to give me part of the registration number of the merc that was seen on the Hobfield," said Ruth. "It's MTE. Erskine's initials?"

"Again, not enough. Driving through the Hobfield Estate is not a crime," Calladine said. "I'll go and have another chat with Newton. See if I can talk some sense into him."

"Want me to come?" asked Ruth.

Calladine shook his head. "No. Hope you hadn't forgotten that we're going out tonight. Get off home and get ready. I'll pick you up at eight."

"Enjoy!" Rocco said with a smirk.

"According to the boss, it's work." Ruth smiled. "We're going hobnobbing with the great and good of Leesworth. See what we can find out."

* * *

"We've had Joanna Fox in for questioning," Calladine began. "You must know her. She's close to Erskine. He got her a solicitor, but that was about it. Think about it.

You all work for Erskine, obey his every word, but when it comes down to it, he doesn't give a stuff what happens to you."

Danny 'Newt' Newton looked at the floor. "Who's Erskine?"

"Still pretending you don't know him, eh?" Calladine smiled. "You're trying my patience, Danny. Your mate saw sense. Now things'll go easier for him." Newt looked up. "He's not afraid. He's quite safe. No one can get to him."

Newt grunted. "No one's safe. What did Flake tell you anyway?"

"The truth. He told us about the man in the big car you're always meeting up with. We now have its registration number."

Newton's eyes blazed with anger. "You're lying! Flake knows nowt. You know nowt either."

"Tell us about Erskine. What you did for him. I don't understand why you're so loyal to the man. If things were the other way round, he'd throw you to the wolves."

Newton stared back at him, silent, a sullen expression on his face.

"Okay, have it your way. I've got to go. There's an event on tonight. Erskine'll be there. Shall I say hello from you?" Calladine stood up.

"When do I get out? You can't keep me here much longer. I know my rights."

"There's no rush, Danny. You'll be with us for a while yet. Those workers you used, they identified you from the photo we showed them."

* * *

"I don't understand why he won't talk to us, guv," Rocco said, frowning.

"That's down to Erskine and his reputation. Newton believes that if he talks, he's a dead man."

"This do tonight. Will Erskine be there?" Rocco asked.

"I hope so, Rocco. I hope he takes his partner along too. I can't wait to see his face." Calladine and Rocco went into the office to find Alice back at her desk.

"Sir!" Alice called. "I'm here because the doc got back. He's emailing you a copy of his own log entry for the evidence thing. There was a contact lens found on one of the bodies, but it didn't belong to the victim. It was bagged up and placed in the evidence store ready for DNA testing. But it disappeared."

Calladine remembered the altered entry she'd shown him. "Have the tech boys been able to do anything with the one in the original log?"

"No," she said. "The paper was too worn."

"The doc is absolutely certain about what he told you?"

"Yes. There was quite a stink about it at the time. DCI Boyd was taken to task. The doc says it was eventually decided that the bag containing the lens was lost in transit between the lab and the evidence store."

Calladine doubted that. After what Marilyn Fallon had told him earlier, he had a good idea who had taken the lens, and why.

"Okay, Alice, good work. Get off home now."

"If it's okay, sir, I'll stay a bit longer. I want to write up my report on what the doc told me."

"Not too late, mind." He smiled at her. Alice was keen. Calladine liked that. She was shaping up to be a really useful member of the team.

He sat at Ruth's desk and stared at the incident board. Miles Erskine was their main suspect. They knew he was responsible for the drugs, but could they prove it? There were a dozen or more texts on Eve's phone but all of them short, a few words only. They had discussed the details in person. The fact that Erskine worked with someone who was party to his kidnap might not hold up either. Joanna Fox hadn't denied her involvement, but had insisted she'd been coerced by persons unknown. Then there were the murders, including the one that Norbury had been imprisoned for. If Erskine was the killer, why wait all these years? Serial murderers didn't kill in fits and starts like this one. One murder twenty years ago and two recently — that didn't fit any pattern Calladine had ever heard of.

He stood up. He was doing no good here. He should go home and get ready. A good lawyer would make mincemeat out of what they had. They needed a lot more.

Chapter 39

Alice was busy at her desk with the office lights dimmed. She heard the door open and looked up. Superintendent Ford was standing in the entrance. He was wearing a dark suit and a bowtie, obviously dressed to go out for the evening.

"Can I help you, sir?" Alice was nervous. She hadn't spoken to him before.

"Calladine?"

"He's gone now, sir." Alice didn't say where. She wasn't sure why, but something stopped her.

"How is the case progressing?"

"The drugs side of things is going well. With regard to the murders, we have forensic evidence being analysed which should give us a name for whoever killed the two women."

"Forensic evidence?"

He sounded surprised. Alice stared at him. Wasn't that their job? What did he think they did all day? "Yes, sir, taken from the second body."

"How did that happen? I was told the killer was careful not to leave a single trace."

Did he sound angry? No, that couldn't be right.

"Not this time, sir," she said. "Our second victim fought back. She bit him. There was evidence between her teeth."

Ford was staring at her. His lips moved. Alice got the distinct impression that he was struggling to frame a question.

"This evidence will all be at the Duggan, I expect. In the safekeeping of Professor Batho?"

"Yes, sir. The professor is working flat out in order to get the results quickly. He's aware of how important it is."

"Good. The team's hard work should yield fruit very soon in that case. I'll leave you to it. There is somewhere I have to be." He turned and strode away.

Alice didn't know what to make of the conversation. But one thing she did know — she didn't like the man. She retrieved her mobile from her bag and rang Calladine. No answer. She'd try him again later.

* * *

Ruth looked in the wardrobe mirror and studied her reflection, head tilted. She supposed she'd do. The royal blue dress fitted her perfectly. A little make-up, lip gloss, her hair brushed into its usual shiny bob, and she was ready.

"I won't be late," she told Jake. She nodded at Harry, who was playing with his toys. "Don't stand any nonsense off that one. Bottle and bed, a quick story, then leave him to it."

He looked up at her, frowning. "I did think we might talk tonight."

"We'd just be going over the same old ground, Jake. I don't see the point. You know how I feel."

"The day is fast approaching when I get in the car and drive away from here with all my belongings in the boot. What will you do then, Ruth? What about me living and working in Sussex, and you doing the same up here? How do we fix that?"

"We're not there yet," she said.

"You're going to have to face it soon. We have one huge problem."

Ruth was about to answer when the doorbell rang. It was Calladine.

"Just in time to stop another blazing row," she whispered, leading the way into the sitting room.

"I'm off," Ruth said. She picked up Harry and kissed him on the cheek. "Be a good boy for Daddy."

* * *

Jake kept his eyes fixed on the TV screen. Calladine nodded at him, but there was no response. This was the first time he'd seen Jake like this. Ordinarily, he'd have chatted about the football, something on the news, any old thing. This just wasn't him.

He followed Ruth out to the car. "I think Jake sees me as the problem. He probably thinks I'm the one influencing you to stay."

"Don't you flatter yourself. He knows damn well what the problem is. I don't want to go."

"Because of the job?" Calladine asked.

"Yes, but more than that. I was born in this area. I have friends here, family." She turned and looked at him. "Why? Don't you want me to stay? Perhaps you'd like to get rid of me. Get yourself a new partner."

Calladine grinned. "Now there's an idea. One who isn't so lippy, for a start!"

"Sorry, Tom. I didn't mean it. But you see how it is. Jake is moody. He wants it all his own way. I really don't think he cares about me anymore."

"You're wrong," Calladine said. "He loves you. He just doesn't know what to do."

"When did you get so wise?"

"Around the time I got so old," he said. "Sorry, but we have to talk tactics now."

"Tactics won't work with Jake," Ruth said.

"No, I mean for tonight. We mix and mingle. If Erskine is there, I want you to talk to him. He doesn't know you. Lead the conversation, talk about local events. Get the measure of the man, and see what you can shake out."

"Given what we know about him, that's a big ask," Ruth said. "I'm pretty nervous. A big function like this, it's not my usual midweek pastime, you know."

"You'll be fine, Ruth. Think of it as research. We'll watch Erskine, note who he talks to, listen to what he says. We still have a number of questions still unanswered."

"We're here," she said. The Leesworth Hall Hotel was a vast, palatial building, right in the centre of Lowermill. "Deep breath, and in we go. Why do I feel as if we're entering the dragon's lair?"

He smiled at her. "I feel the same way."

* * *

Eve rushed over to them the minute they walked in. She looked relieved to see Calladine. "This is torture. After what's been going on, it's the last thing I wanted to do. Word has got round that my factory was involved, and everyone keeps asking me what happened. What do I tell them?"

"Nothing. We haven't put the case to bed yet." Calladine bent down and kissed her cheek. "Tonight, it's work for Ruth and me. We want to meet folk. Is Erskine here?"

"Miles? Yes, he is. He's over there."

Calladine saw the puzzled look on her face. She didn't know about his involvement yet. "Take Ruth over and introduce her. Don't mention that she's CID. I'm sure that'll come out later."

Calladine looked around. There was someone in particular he wanted to see tonight. And there he was, glass in hand, staring out of the large bay windows. Superintendent Angus Ford.

Calladine made his move. "Hello, sir. Good turnout."

He saw the look of surprise. "I suppose your presence is down to her?" Ford nodded towards Eve.

Calladine laughed. "If by 'her,' you mean my mother, then yes. A mere DI like me would hardly get an invite any other way. It looks like the crème de la crème of Leesworth are here tonight."

Ford snorted. "Not so sure about that. Charlatans and villains, a lot of them."

"Ah, I see what you mean. There's one over there, talking to my sergeant. Miles Erskine hides it well, but he's fast running out of luck." Calladine intended the observation to annoy, and it worked. There was an instant response.

"Miles is no villain! He's a close friend of mine."

"Sorry, I forgot. The pair of you are a couple these days, aren't you? Have been for decades in fact, if the gossip is correct."

Ford was evidently struggling to keep his temper. "I don't see what that has to do with you or anyone else. You'd do well to keep your snide remarks to yourself, Calladine."

"Ordinarily I'd agree with you, sir, but you see, Miles Erskine is a person of interest in our current case."

"How so? What do you imagine Miles has been up to?" Ford turned and made for the bar, Calladine following.

"Drugs, kidnap, murder . . . The list is growing."

Ford came to an abrupt halt. He spun round and stared at Calladine, his face red with fury.

"How dare you!"

Calladine stood with his hands in his trouser pockets, casually regarding his opponent. "We are within a spit of getting a confession from a young man we have in custody. We have Erskine's car registration, a log of phone calls and texts. The DNA results from evidence we gathered at the scene will confirm it. I'm afraid things are looking bleak for your Mr Erskine." He smiled at Ford. "You might like to give some thought to your own position, sir. We arrest Erskine and it won't look good for you." Calladine turned and walked away.

He heard his mobile ring, and found a small ante-room where he could take the call.

It was Julian Batho. "There's been a break-in at the Duggan."

That wasn't something that happened every day. Security at the Duggan was tight. It had blanket CCTV coverage and a small army of security guards.

"Anything taken?"

"Fortunately not. The perpetrators, two masked men, were after the evidence gathered from your two murders. They threatened one of the guards and demanded to know its whereabouts. He took them along to the store. It wasn't there. The evidence is currently undergoing tests in my lab, and that is locked up tight."

"What did they do then? No one got hurt, I hope."

"The alarm was raised and they were arrested. The pair of them have been taken to Leesdon."

"Thanks for letting me know, Julian."

"We've now completed all the tests on the samples. The DNA extracted from between the teeth is not that of your victims. That means I have a complete DNA profile for your killer."

This was the breakthrough Calladine had been hoping for, but he wasn't sure if Erskine's DNA was on record. "Does it match any on the database?"

Julian paused for a moment. "I'm sorry, Tom. No."

Chapter 40

"Ruth and Miles appear to have hit it off," Eve said with a smile. "I heard the pair of them laughing, and he's just ordered another bottle of champagne. I think they're out on the terrace."

Calladine went to join them. The two of them were sitting at a table with another couple. Erskine looked his affable best — joking, and pouring drinks for everyone.

"Come and join us, Calladine," he said. "You know Ruth, I believe. She's a colleague of yours, in fact. We've been discussing that piece of land by the canal I've been after for development. She's explained that there's water fowl nesting there, so I've got to wait. Looks like another project of mine down the tubes."

Calladine sat down beside Ruth. "Things bad, Mr Erskine? Is that why you've branched out recently?"

"You won't rile me, Inspector. I'm not Angus. You really shouldn't wind him up like that. He has a short fuse, you know. He's likely to blow a gasket."

"I wonder what he'll do to protect you this time?"

Erskine laughed. "He doesn't need to protect me from anything. I mess up, I clean up that mess. Always have, always will. I don't rely on others to watch my back."

The couple who'd been sitting with Erskine and Ruth got up and went inside. "You won't get away with it this time," Calladine said. "We've made further arrests tonight. They'll talk, as will the two lads we already have in custody. They'll soon see sense and tell us the lot."

"Rubbish. I've done nothing."

"The evidence is building. You need to watch your step." Calladine took Ruth's arm, and they left Erskine sitting alone at the table.

"I saw Ford earlier," Ruth said. "Made me nervous as a kitten. It's the way he looks at you. He's weird."

"Ford is the one Marilyn told me about — Erskine's partner. It's Ford who's been watching that villain's back all these years. I bet it was Ford who took that lens too, all those years ago."

"That's really big, Tom. You can't do anything with the information unless you can prove it. Do you think Erskine is responsible for the Norbury killing as well?"

"Yes, I do. I think Ford made sure of the outcome. He worked in the background on that case, as did I. But he could easily have influenced both the events and Norbury."

"You still need proof, Tom."

Calladine sighed. "I know, and it's doing my head in."

"What now? Are we leaving the party?"

"Two thugs have had a go at the Duggan. They've been arrested. I want to interview them as soon as I can."

Ruth checked her watch. "It's nearly ten p.m., you know."

"You can go home if you want. I can do it without you."

"I'll come. But I do feel a little overdressed for an interview."

Calladine laughed. "I'd say underdressed actually, given that neckline."

Ruth slapped his arm. "Cheeky sod. Your phone is ringing again, by the way."

They got into his car while he took the call. It was Alice.

"I rang you earlier but you didn't answer," she said. "By the time I got home, my mobile was dead, hence the time it's taken me to get back. It might be nothing, sir, but I can't get it out of my head. Just after you left, Superintendent Ford came into the incident room. He asked about the cases. I told him where we were up to and he seemed particularly interested in the evidence we'd collected."

"And I know why," Calladine said. "There's been an attempted robbery at the Duggan. They were after that evidence of ours."

"You think that was down to Ford?" Alice said.

"Can't say yet, but leave it with us. With a bit of luck, we should have the whole lot wrapped up soon. Julian now has the DNA profile we so badly needed." He ended the call and turned to Ruth. "They're panicking, Erskine and Ford. Tonight's botched attempt proves that."

"We still need someone to talk to us, Tom. A few words, and then we can haul Erskine in."

* * *

The two men had been put in separate cells. Calladine checked the arresting officer's paperwork and then had a quick peek at each of them.

"The one in cell five, the tall, skinny one. Do we know him?"

"Liam Rawlins, sir. Been at it for years. He's been here before, and done time. Do anything for money that one. But these days he drinks and talks too much. I'm surprised the villains of this parish still use him."

"Perhaps they were desperate. Couldn't find anyone else at short notice." Calladine looked at Ruth. "I'll do this with one of the uniforms. You wait in the incident room."

"Shout if you need help. Go in there and nail him."

"Right, Mr Rawlins," Calladine began. "What were you after at the Duggan Centre?"

"Stuff."

"You surprise me. They've nothing of value in there, nothing you can sell. Did someone put you up to it?"

"Like who?"

"I don't know. Go on, surprise me." Calladine sat back and regarded him. Liam Rawlins was rough looking, spoke in a gruff voice and coughed constantly. This could be the joker who'd threatened him on his street.

"If you don't talk to me, you'll have to stay with us, I'm afraid. Now you don't want that, do you? I'm sure you've got far better things to do."

"Look, copper, whatever this is, it's got nowt to do with me. I was just helping out a mate. Said he had some stuff to shift."

"Rubbish! Someone put you up to it." Calladine leaned forward. "A bit of a rush job. Had to be done tonight. Am I right? Do yourself a favour. Tell me who put you up to it." Calladine watched Rawlins struggle with this.

"He warned me off. Said if the coppers got curious, I was to keep shtum."

"It's up to you, Liam, but the man who put you up to it is going down himself."

Rawlins coughed. "I was having a pint in the Wellington when I gets this call. Someone I do the odd job for wants me to get stuff from that lab."

"Name?"

"Can't say. It's slipped my mind." Rawlins said.

"Okay, have it your way. You can take the rap for drug dealing and possibly murder. Want that, do you? Talk to me and I can help you. Refuse, and you are in the frame for a list as long as your arm."

"I ain't killed anyone," Rawlins said.

Calladine said nothing, watching him shift uncomfortably on the chair.

"I'm not taking the blame for anything other than the robbery tonight. And we didn't get 'owt. Done up like Fort Knox that place. Erskine should've said."

"Erskine? Would that be Miles Erskine?"

Rawlins coughed again, and nodded. "Rang me. Said the job was urgent. Told me to get some samples from the lab and destroy them."

"He'll be upset that you didn't do the job, Liam. You're going to need us to look after you for a while."

"Too bloody true. Erskine ain't someone you cross."

"You'll be fine. We won't let anything happen to you." Calladine stood up. "You will give my colleague here a comprehensive statement. Then we'll make you comfortable for the night." He looked at the officer. "Get him a cup of tea."

* * *

Calladine returned to the incident room, jubilant. "We've got him! I'm about to return to that hotel and bring Erskine in."

"Want me to come with you?" Ruth asked.

"No. I'll take a couple of uniforms with me. You go home. There'll be plenty to do in the morning."

"Ford won't be pleased."

"Nothing he can do. We have one of Erskine's little helpers in custody, and he's spilling his guts. Tomorrow we'll get a search warrant for that office of his. In the meantime, I'm going to post a uniform on guard there, just in case."

"What's bothering you?"

"The possibility that Erskine used his office phone to ring Eve. She told me there were many calls. The man isn't infallible. He might easily have slipped up. If he did, we'll check the dates and times of the calls against Eve's mobile data."

"Are you going to tell Birch? This is going to affect Ford. She won't be pleased if you've kept her in the dark."

Calladine checked the clock. It was getting late. "I'll have to, I suppose. But I'll go get Erskine first."

* * *

"I thought you'd left," Eve said. People still thronged the rooms, jostling and talking loudly.

"Is Erskine still here?" Calladine asked.

"He's in the bar with Angus Ford."

"Come on." Calladine beckoned to the two uniformed officers and they wound their way through the partygoers.

Calladine had to shout above the chatter. "Mr Erskine. I need you to come down to the station and answer a few questions."

"At this time of night? Don't be ridiculous." Erskine turned his back.

"You're joking," Ford said. "What do you think Miles has done?"

Calladine counted the charges on his fingers. "Drugs, kidnap, murder . . . That'll do for starters."

Ford's face turned red. "You're testing my patience, Calladine."

Calladine ignored him. "Earlier this evening, there was an attempted break-in at the Duggan. One of those involved has just told me you put him up to it, Erskine."

"He's lying." Erskine's back was still turned.

"Nonetheless, I have questions."

"Can't it wait till tomorrow?" Ford said. "Really. All this fuss on the say-so of some small-time villain."

"They were after the evidence gathered from the body of our second murder victim. For that reason, I can't let it pass. I have to take what I've been told seriously." Calladine waited.

Erskine looked at Ford and nodded. "Don't worry, Angus. My lawyer will have me out in no time."

Angry. Calladine recalled Ford's look from the old days, and the name he'd given him.

"You will speak to DCI Birch when you get to the station. Ask her to come in. I'll have a word with her."

Chapter 41

Day 8

It had been a long night. Erskine kept insisting he'd done nothing. First thing the next morning, Calladine had a DNA swab taken from him and rushed it to Julian.

"Rocco, take Alice and speak to Newton again. Tell him that Erskine's in custody. Let's see where that takes us. Has the warrant come through for the search on his premises?" Calladine said.

Rocco nodded. "Yes, sir, we're on it."

"Ruth, as soon as Rocco has finished, get round there. In the meantime, have Erskine's office sealed off."

DCI Birch strode into the room. "Calladine! I hear you've arrested Miles Erskine."

"Not yet, ma'am. That'll come later this morning, with luck. For the time being he's helping with enquiries."

"Don't bandy words with me. I've also just learned that he is Ford's partner. Ford has been on the phone. He's livid."

"We have testimony from a witness who's told us that Erskine hired him to break into the Duggan. What am I supposed to do? Ignore it because he lives with the chief super?" Calladine could see she wasn't happy, but he was right. There was nothing she could do. She gave him a filthy look and stormed off.

Rocco stuck his head round the door. "Newton wants to make a statement. Better than that, he's told us where Erskine stores the drugs. He uses one of his own buildings at the industrial estate."

"You and Ruth get down there. Ask CSI to meet you. I think it's time I had a word with Miles Erskine."

* * *

Erskine was sitting with his lawyer, drinking tea. "I've been here all night," he said. "You really do need to beef up the accommodation. The mattresses aren't up to much."

Calladine ignored the comment. "Danny Newton has finally spoken to us. He's told us all about your shady little enterprise."

Erskine turned pale. "He knows nothing."

"He knows enough to enable me to charge you. We're currently searching your premises. We know where you keep the drugs. We'll find them very soon. We'll also be taking a look at your office phone records. Let's hope you didn't slip up and use it for your nasty little sideline."

Erskine seemed to deflate. "I employ a lot of people, they take liberties, use my premises for their own ends. The drugs you say you're looking for could have been put there by anyone. That villain you've got in custody would say anything to save his skin. Even go as far as blackening my name. You're clutching at straws, Calladine."

"I don't think so. The evidence is building. Later today we will have enough to charge you."

This appeared to upset him. Erskine was nervous, his face pale.

"You should come clean while you can. Given the evidence I'm sure your solicitor would agree."

"I still think you're bluffing. You have very little solid evidence against me."

"We have DNA from one of the murder victims. We will test that against the sample taken from you this morning. We expect the sample to match."

Erskine said simply, "It won't." Erskine's eyes met Calladine's. "I didn't kill anyone. Not now and not in the past."

"You're lying." Calladine was adamant.

"I'm telling you the truth."

Calladine shook his head. He didn't believe him.

Erskine fell silent, seeming to wrestle with something. Something about Ford.

"Over the years I've done everything I can to help that man. I can't continue, this is the end. Part of me always knew it would come to this. I have warned Angus often enough." He looked at Calladine across the table. "Alright. I hold my hands up. You are going to find the evidence anyway, the drugs, the phone records. I did organise the manufacture of the drugs. I had you kidnapped. I also admit that you might not have been allowed to return. For a number of reasons, we had to get you out of the way. Your relationship with Eve Buckley, the fact that you are a detective . . . plus, Angus wanted it that way."

Calladine looked at him. "The murders? Ford can't help you now."

"Angus? What makes you think he would help me?"

"Because he's been cleaning up after you for years. Stealing evidence, bullying and coaching suspects. In short, all this time he's been making sure that you've been kept out of trouble. If it weren't for him you'd have been put away a whole lot sooner."

Erskine gave a hollow laugh. "You've got this totally wrong."

Calladine stared at him. Erskine sounded so confident, like a man telling the truth. "In that case, explain it to me."

"*I* am the one who has done the 'cleaning up,' as you put it. For years I've been protecting Angus." Erskine looked down at his hands, and then at his solicitor. He took a breath. "Angus is your killer."

Angus Ford, a murderer? Calladine stared at Erskine. The look on the man's face said it all. He wasn't lying. It seemed so obvious now. Yet it was hard to believe that a top police officer had carried out such horrific crimes. "The Norbury killing?" Calladine asked.

Erskine nodded. "That too."

"Why the gap? The first was twenty years ago, and now two more?"

The look Erskine gave him made Calladine's blood run cold. "There was no gap. I clean up after this man, remember. I've been hiding his dirty little secrets for years."

Calladine almost whispered, "How many?"

"Last time I counted, there were six. You can see for yourselves. Angus always films each kill. You'll find all the tapes at our house."

"What did you do with the bodies? Give us names if you can recall them."

"If I can't, Angus will. He talks about them in his sleep."

Epilogue

Calladine gathered the team together in the incident room and gave them the whole story.

"Ford? But he's one of us!" Rocco said. "Has he been arrested?"

"Too true, he has. CSI are going through their house now. As Erskine said, Ford made videos and we have them," Calladine said. "With Erskine's collusion, Ford has been killing women for years. No one suspected either of them. One was the respected business man, the other a detective with his sights set on a top job. Soon we'll have the results from Ford's DNA test. I expect it to match that of our second victim."

"Poor George Norbury," Ruth said. "Such a shame he had to spend his last years inside."

"Ford admitted to beating him, and to the coaching. He promised Norbury that the sentence wouldn't be a long one."

"And Norbury never complained," Ruth said.

"Once he was inside, Erskine's lot were threatening him."

"What a case," Ruth said. "It's worn me out. Why did they kidnap you?"

"They needed an out-of-the-way spot and a ready supply of chemicals to manufacture the drugs. The rambling outbuildings at Buckley's provided that. Buckley's was chosen because of Eve and her relationship to me. Ford needed to get me out of the way. He knew I'd compare the first killing of Ingrid Plesec to the Norbury one and become suspicious."

"Except it wasn't Norbury at all, poor man. We should stop calling it that," Ruth said.

Calladine nodded. "The so-called tipoff was set up, and the rest you know."

Ruth yawned. "This is one case I'm more than happy to put to bed."

Calladine checked the time. It was mid-afternoon. "Let's call it a day and go across to the Wheatsheaf."

That was a universally popular idea. The team collected their things and made their way out.

Calladine joined Ruth on the stairs. "It's Friday. D-Day for Jake's job. What have you decided?"

"I'm not going." Her voice was firm.

"You can't let him go on his own. That'll be the end. You two belong together, Ruth."

"Give over, Calladine. I'll do what I bloody well want. Jake has a choice to make. He'll phone me later with his decision."

"Rocco was telling me you met another nice young man a couple of days ago — that forensic artist the Duggan sent round."

Ruth nodded. "Michael, yes. He seems okay. We'll use him again, I'm sure."

"Rocco told me there was a spark between the two of you."

Ruth laughed. "Rocco has a vivid imagination. Even if Jake does bugger off, that doesn't mean I'm in the market for another man."

"Don't mess up like me, Ruth. I don't seem capable of keeping up a solid, long-term relationship, but you're different."

"You really are a worrier, aren't you? We're here. Come on, happy face now." Ruth nudged him. "And get your hand in your pocket. The team deserve it."

Ruth's mobile rang. "Get me a large red. I'll join you when I've taken this."

Calladine bought the drinks and ushered the others to a table. He looked through the window at Ruth pacing up and down the pavement outside. He didn't need telling. This was it. It had to be Jake.

Then she was back. "Bloody fool." She picked up her drink and took a big swallow.

The team had their eyes glued on her. Like Calladine, they knew she was waiting for Jake's call.

"Stop it you lot, you're making me nervous." She grinned. "All that fuss, all those arguments, and look what happens."

"What?" Calladine asked. "They don't want him to start sooner, do they? Come on, you can't keep us in suspense."

Ruth gave him a broad smile. "They don't want him at all. It's a private school. Turns out it has dire financial problems. As of today, it's closing its doors for the foreseeable future."

"What does that mean for Jake?" Rocco asked.

"Don't you get it, dozy?" Ruth ruffled his hair. "No school, no job, and therefore no move. Problem sorted. Good, eh?"

THE END

Thank you for reading this book. If you enjoyed it please leave feedback on Amazon, and if there is anything we missed or you have a question about then please get in touch. The author and publishing team appreciate your feedback and time reading this book.

Our email is office@joffebooks.com

www.joffebooks.com

ALSO BY HELEN H. DURRANT

CALLADINE & BAYLISS
Book 1: DEAD WRONG
Book 2: DEAD SILENT
Book 3: DEAD LIST
Book 4: DEAD LOST
Book 5: DEAD & BURIED
Book 6: DEAD NASTY
Book 7: DEAD JEALOUS
Book 8: DEAD BAD

THE DCI GRECO BOOKS
Book 1: DARK MURDER
Book 2: DARK HOUSES
Book 3: DARK TRADE
Book4: DARK ANGEL

DI MATT BRINDLE
HIS THIRD VICTIM

37537102R00148

Printed in Poland
by Amazon Fulfillment
Poland Sp. z o.o., Wrocław